THE POWER OF FATE

THE POWER OF FATE

THE TRIAD SERIES, BOOK 5

KATE PEARCE

1

———

"MYA, PAY ATTENTION!"

"I *am*..." Her breath hissed out as Orin expertly kicked with his bare foot, caught her shoulder, and sent her flying backward onto the black exercise mat.

He came down over her, the side of his hand slicing across her throat. "You'd be dead now if this were real."

She grinned up at him. "But it isn't, and you wouldn't kill me."

His expression remained serious. "This isn't funny. I'm trying to make sure you are one hundred percent ready to go on this mission."

"This was supposed to be fun." She shoved at his chest, but he didn't budge a centimeter. "Orin..."

After a second he rolled off her and stalked over to the side of the mat. "I picked up another shift tonight. I need to go shower."

For a long, stunned moment, Mya remained on her back staring up at the ceiling before following Orin up the stairs to the bathroom in their apartment. Clouds of steam issued out of the shower.

"Hey."

He was naked and just about to step into the shower.

"You're going out on my last night home?" She tried to keep her tone light, but she had an absurd desire to cry. He stepped under the water, and she focused on his assured movements as he lathered himself with soap and washed his short black hair.

"Orin..."

She sank down onto the side of the bath as he ignored her. Tentatively, she probed his mind, but his shields were up. It was like scraping her fingernails against a metal door. They'd been mated for ten years. What the frak was happening?

"Please talk to me, Orin."

He kept his back to her and his mind closed. Wearily, she got up and went to the spare bedroom and showered there. She was quick because she was not going to allow him to leave without talking to her properly. Wrapping the towel around herself, she went back into their bedroom where he was dressing in his city police uniform. She took a deep breath.

"Is there someone else?"

He stopped moving but kept his back to her. "Mya, that's stupid. We're mated. I don't do casual sex."

"So you're just tired of me?"

He slowly turned. "I'm tired of this distance between us."

"You're the one who put it there, Orin."

He pulled a thin protective vest over his black T-shirt, his movements jerky and impatient. "Do you really want to do this just before you leave on a mission?"

"Why not?" She raised her chin. "Better than leaving things to fester. Maybe being away will give me a chance to think about what's wrong and work out how *I* feel. I don't *want* to fight with you."

"You don't want to fight about anything. You're Hakron. You think everything can be sorted out with prayer and goodwill."

"Even though I chose to join the military, there's nothing

wrong with promoting peace. It has prevented bloodshed in my tribe for hundreds of years."

He sank down on the side of the bed and stared at his booted feet. "We've been mated for a decade."

She nodded even though he wasn't looking at her. "And?"

"You won't talk about changing that. I want to take you to the Temple at Quoxor and find out who our Third is." He looked up, his blue gaze utterly serious. "I want a child."

Only mated Triads could conceive children on their planet. And only the Oracle could sanction a bonded Triad—not that Mya was sure that she'd ever be ready for a child.

"But we agreed that we'd wait until both our careers were stable, and this mission is crucial to me proving I'm the obvious choice to take over for Major Esca." She was almost stuttering in her haste to remind him. "We discussed this. I thought you *agreed* with me."

"That was before all this shit went down at work." His throat worked. "Before Kran died."

Mya sank down to her knees in front of him. "Losing your partner like that was horrible, Orin."

"It made me think. What if I go next? I'd be leaving you alone and without even a child to remember me by." He held up his hand. "And don't tell me you'd manage—that you'd be fine without me. I know that. You're a strong woman."

"You make it sound as if I wouldn't miss you at all." Mia's words stuck in her throat. "I'm your mate. I'd be *devastated*. You make it sound like I don't care."

"I don't mean that." He shoved a hand through his now spiky hair. "This is about *me*, not you. *I've* changed. I *know* what we said—what we agreed. And I know you're frightened. All I'm asking you to do is think about it, okay? If you don't want a child—maybe, just maybe, our Third might?"

She remained kneeling, staring at nothing as her carefully

constructed world collapsed around her. If she wouldn't give him a child he'd get one another way.

Without her.

With a Third.

Yeah, and that always worked out *so* well...

"I do love you, Mya. In a perfect world, all I'd want is a child with you. You are my heart." Orin spoke so quietly she almost couldn't hear him.

She closed her eyes and took a deep breath. She would not fight with him. She would *not*. "I love you, too. Keep safe tonight. When I get back, I promise we can talk about this some more."

"That's—" He paused as relief flooded his even features. "*Thank you.* Thank you so much. If we did have a child, I'd stay home with it and our Third, I wouldn't expect you to be at home if you wanted to stay in the military."

Pushing her out, making her obsolete to his happiness... "You've obviously thought about this quite a bit."

He shrugged. "I had a lot of time when I was stuck in that hospital bed recovering."

She managed a nod. It was pretty much all she could dredge up at this moment. His wrist com beeped and he cursed.

"Gotta go."

"Okay," Mya whispered. "Take care of yourself and come back safely to me."

"I'll do my best." His com beeped again. Ignoring it, he put his hands on her shoulders. "I love you, Mya. Please don't forget that. I want what's best for both of us, not just me, I swear it."

She nodded again as his mind reached for hers, and for a long moment, their thoughts tangled and blended until he eased back.

"Maybe I should call in sick," he murmured as he cupped her cheek. "I don't want to leave you. I'm a frakking idiot to have started this right now."

"I'm good." She summoned another smile. "Really. I have to leave in less than two hours, so you might as well go and earn that overtime."

"Are you sure?"

Leaning in, she kissed his firm mouth. "Yes. Go. Be well."

He reluctantly let her go, his worried blue gaze fixed on hers as he picked up his heavy jacket and backed toward the door. "I love you. Stay safe, you hear?"

"Shouldn't be a problem. This is just an escort mission."

"To an Etruscan moon. So be careful."

"I always am."

"Which is why you'll get that promotion." He blew her a kiss. "Let me know how things are going when you can."

"Will do."

She stayed where she was until the door of their apartment slammed behind him. There was no point hanging around feeling sorry for herself. She might as well get to the base and prepare for the mission ahead. Most of her gear was already packed. She just needed to put on her uniform.

She went to get up and couldn't; her arms wrapped around her waist as tears fell in an endless stream. Gods it *hurt*. She used her towel to mop up the storm of weeping and tried to talk herself into a better frame of mind. Orin wanted to find their Third and have a child, which was totally natural and understandable.

Both of those things *terrified* her.

He *knew* that. At least some of it.

It was her fault for starting the whole damn conversation. She'd practically begged him to tell her what was wrong. Just because she didn't like his answer didn't make Orin's feelings any less valid or important. At least he'd tried to be honest with her.

He did love her. She knew that in her soul.

Usually, getting dressed in her uniform helped her collect

her thoughts, but tonight it proved impossible. How could she have misinterpreted Orin's increasing withdrawal from her so badly? She was his mate, and yet he'd managed to hide the extent of his feelings for months because she was so busy chasing that promotion.

But he knew how important it was to her, which was probably why he'd hidden his issues so well. If she gained the rank of major she'd be the first Hakron female to ever reach that grade in the Pavlovan Special Forces. She studied her pale green reflection in the mirror. But was her ambition worth losing her best friend and lover over?

If she deliberately stepped back and didn't seek the promotion, would she end up resenting Orin? Could she even *carry* a baby without losing her mind during the pregnancy? She didn't know. And the thought of a Third... Shouldering her pack, she headed for the door. All she could do was honor her promise to Orin, think things through while she was away, and come back ready to have another honest discussion. She hadn't told him how bad things really were in her family because it was still too painful to talk about. Perhaps it was time to trust him with all of it.

She loved him. She'd promised him she'd try.

There was nothing more important than that.

<hr>

AN HOUR LATER, she was at the military base checking in with her team when her superior officer stepped out of his office and called her name.

"Captain Jong?"

Mya saluted. "Yes, sir?"

"Do you have a moment?"

She followed Major Esca into his office and shut the door. He took his seat behind the desk and folded his hands in front of him. Her superior officer was paler than usual, the bags under his eyes more pronounced. Even his black hair had dulled. Worn to the bone—exactly as could be expected from a man whose mate had been injured. Mya was sure she'd looked the same for the weeks Orin was in the hospital. They all knew that Major Esca's First Male, Ash, who basically ran the Pavlovan Senate, had been injured in an Etruscan attack that had also affected several Hakron villagers. Senator Ash was still recuperating at home, and the Major had been running himself ragged trying to do his job and take care of his mate.

"Jong, I wanted you to be the first to know that I'm leaving this position." A shot of pure adrenaline shook through her as he looked up at her. "I am recommending you for promotion. I can't think of anyone who could fill my shoes as well as you could."

"Thank you, sir." Mya swallowed hard and saluted. This was what she'd been working so hard to achieve, and his words gave her immense satisfaction. But the thought that she was achieving her goal because her superior officer's mate was suffering didn't sit well with her. "That is very good of you."

"I can't guarantee you'll get the job, but with my connections, it's pretty damn likely."

Mya tried to smile. "May I ask what you intend to do next, sir?"

Major Esca sat back and stretched out his legs. "When Senator Ash is recovered, I'm going to be spearheading the development of a new security team to protect the leaders of our Senate. We've had too many close calls recently—what with the attack on the Temple at Quoxor, the attempted abduction of the Oracle, *and* the bringing down of Senator Ash's plane."

"The Etruscans are definitely getting bolder."

"And we're going to have to consider what to do about that on a larger scale soon. No one wants an outright war, but these acts of aggression are getting out of hand."

"Agreed, sir."

"The mission we are about to undertake is twofold. There is a diplomatic side where our ambassador is going to lay it on the line to the Etruscans, and there is a 'fact gathering' element. While I'm facing off with the Etruscans and trying to keep my temper, you and your team will be assessing the Etruscan moon. We've never been close enough to get a good sense of it before, let alone been allowed on the surface, and it could be strategically important if we do end up at war."

"Understood."

"You will be discreet and invisible."

"Aren't I always, sir?"

His smile was more like his old self. "I'm relying on that. Be careful, Jong."

2

Mya paused at the edge of the clearing to reset her position. Her headset registered a single click from each of the other three team members. They were only communicating telepathically when absolutely necessary, because the Etruscans did have some trained telepaths in their military.

She gazed down at the entrance to an unknown structure set beneath a small rise in the ground and then scanned the maps Major Esca had sent her. The buildings weren't marked— although there was some kind of residence noted on the other side of the forest, which was within the same land boundary. She couldn't decide if the building was military or not, but it did appear to be guarded.

The cracking sound of a twig behind her was all the warning she got before something hit her from behind and sent her crashing forward into the undergrowth.

"You are awake."

Mya cautiously opened one eye and found she was sitting on

her ass with her back propped against the wall of a small cell. There was a man dressed in the uniform of the Etruscan Imperial Guard sitting on a chair in front of her, which couldn't be good. She tried to lick her lips, aware that her head was throbbing and that she was thirsty.

"Captain Jong, isn't it?" The officer's contemptuous gaze swept over her. "I've heard about telepathic mutants on your planet with colored skin. I never realized they'd let you into their *military*. I suppose, knowing the immoral nature of their telepathic society, they probably think it's being progressive."

"Why am I here?"

The man's smile wasn't reassuring. "You'll find out."

"If I am a prisoner, I request you inform either the Pavlovan embassy or my military command."

"You can request anything you like, mutant."

Mya struggled to her feet. "Space protocol in this system allows for the exchange of basic information about prisoners between planetary nations. I ask that you follow convention and do as I have requested."

He sauntered over to her. "The thing is, Jong, you're off the grid. No one knows you are here, and no one cares what happens to you while you are here. Get it?"

She refused to look away. "That is unacceptable. Military code—"

He slapped her face so hard that her head hit the wall behind her.

"Shut up, Jong." He raised his voice. "Amar and Kane, get in here!" He grabbed Mya's arm and pushed her toward the opening door. "Strip her and get her in there right now."

She fought, but the two males were big and neither of them cared if they hurt her as they cut off her uniform, leaving her in her underwear. Just as she feared the worst, they stopped touching her and shoved her through another door, locking it behind her.

She sank down onto a soft floor and blinked at the sudden transformation. The space was painted cream and white and done up like a fancy hotel room. In the center of the room there was a bed containing a single occupant. Gathering her courage, she stood as some strange compulsion came over her to get closer to the still figure.

Telepath.

Gods. The strongest one she had ever encountered. Even stronger than Senator Ash.

She moved closer, her bare feet making no sound on the spongy flooring, her breath the loudest thing in the room. The male drew her like a beam of light in the darkest, deepest tunnel. She could no more have turned away than ceased to exist.

He lay on his back, his blond head turned away from her. There were golden bands around his wrists and ankles and a collar around his neck. Apart from that, he was naked. He was one of the biggest men she had ever seen—his shoulders wide, his waist narrow and his legs going on forever.

Beautiful.

"Sir." She cleared her throat. "I'm Captain Jong of the Pavlovan Special Forces, I—"

"Go away, Jong." His voice was low and held no inflection. "There is nothing for you here."

"But I want to help you, sir. We can help each other."

"Then leave me alone."

She shivered. "I don't think I can." His mind was extraordinary, the power emanating from him so immense that she wanted to warm herself in it.

"You're a telepath, sir?" He didn't answer her. She tried a thought. *"Telepath?"* And caught her breath as his mind repelled hers like broken shards of glass.

She waited another moment, but he continued to pretend she didn't exist.

It took all her strength to retreat from his glorious power to the corner of the room as he'd requested. It was the only thing he'd asked her to do, and she had to respect that. Backing away, she refocused on the rest of her team, but something in her current environment kept bouncing her thoughts back to her. No wonder the Etruscan had seemed confident she wouldn't be missed. The thing was, he didn't know her team. Unless they found her body, they would never give up searching for her.

Or would they? This current mission was a covert one, and diplomatic relations between the two planets were extremely strained. Would Major Esca be prepared to go to war over her? Would she want him to? With a soft moan, she leaned her head against the wall and closed her eyes.

It didn't seem more than a second passed before she was being dragged upright by Kane and Amar and marched over to the bed again. The obnoxious Etruscan officer was also there.

"Jong, you're not cooperating."

She set her jaw and simply stared him down.

"See this male? He needs fucking, and you're going to do it."

She refused to even answer that.

"You're going to do it, Jong, and I'm going to vidscreen it for my superiors." He nodded at her captors. "Hold her still."

She gasped as he stuck her with a syringe, sending something hot rushing into her blood system. Her knees almost gave way as a curious roaring sensation thrummed through her body.

"Wow. How much did you give her, boss?" Amar's voice sounded way too far away. "She's a telepath. I wonder if they react differently?"

"We'll find out. We could be in for a great show."

She was lowered to the floor and left there while the men retreated, her mind scrabbling to make sense of the sparks exploding within her nervous system. Her whole body was convulsed in waves of heat almost as if she were ready to mate, but she'd prevented that with hormone-controlled shots. The imperative to mate and to breed was incredibly strong and hard to overcome. She couldn't—

"Gods…" She curled up into a ball and started crawling back to her corner. If the male hadn't wanted her to touch him earlier, he was not going to want her now when all her senses were alert and she wanted… Oh Gods, she wanted to fuck him senseless.

"Jong."

Even his voice made her shiver with longing.

This was bad. This was *very* bad. She kept moving away from him.

"Captain Jong, listen to me. They've given you something to force you into a mating state."

"No kidding," she muttered through her clenched teeth. "It's okay. I've got this. I'm staying in my corner just like you told me to do."

"*Captain.*"

"Stop talking to me," she hissed. Even his voice made her want him.

She reached the corner. If she turned around and caught even a glimpse of him, she might not be able to stop herself from launching her body on top of his and fucking him hard.

"I'm sorry."

"Shut up!" she whispered and put her fingers in her ears. Yeah, that was going to work. She realized she was rocking back and forth just to ease the agony of need growing in her belly.

For a little while there was silence, and she let herself enjoy it. What would happen if she didn't do what the Etruscan ordered? Would he give her another shot? She moaned and rocked harder, wrapping one arm around her breasts where her nipples were hard points and wedging one hand between her thighs.

"*Jong.*"

"No." Now he wanted a telepathic link? Was he crazy?

"Come to me."

"No. This isn't your fault. I won't use you."

He sighed. *"They'll hurt you. I can't allow that."*

"Not your decision, sir." She tried to shut him out of her mind, but he was too powerful.

After a long while, the door opened again and Mya couldn't help a whimper escaping her lips. The Etruscan officer came over and stared down at her. With a contemptuous smile, he grabbed her by the hair and hauled her to her feet, dragging her back toward the bed.

She could sense the telepath was fully awake now, his body humming with tension. His cock was hard and angling up toward his flat stomach.

"Look at her, telepath. She's fucking gagging for it. The boss wants little baby Pavlovans, so get busy."

"Leave her alone."

"You have a choice, big boy. You fuck her, or we'll all have her right here in front of you and then I'll slit her throat and let her bleed out all over you." He pinched Mya's nipple hard and she flinched away, her gaze locking with the huge male on the bed whose eyes were the same color as his golden shackles.

A muscle flicked in his cheek. "Get out, Nevans."

"Good choice, telepath."

The Etruscan shoved Mya hard enough to make her sprawl on top of the male. The telepath brought up his hands to steady her hips. As soon as he touched her, she forgot everything but the feel of his flesh beneath her own, the hard steel of his cock lodged against her stomach.

"Oh Gods, I'm so *sorry,*" she panted. "I can't seem to help myself."

He stroked her hair. "It's all right. It's not your fault." He didn't seem to be able to stop touching her either, his hands roaming over her ass and hips, pressing her against his muscular frame and the hot stiffness of his shaft. "It's been so long since I've been with my own kind. It's—"

With a groan he found her mouth and kissed her, and she kissed him back. All her common sense was gone, only the need to have him inside her screamed through her head at the most basic, primitive level of need.

"*Yes.*"

He managed to unhook her bra one-handed and then ripped the seam of her panties, yanking them away from her sex as she reared over him and took him deep. Both of them screamed as his big cock worked its way inside her wet and willing sex. She started to come immediately, her body shuddering, demanding more even before the climax ended and getting it, getting every dirty, salacious thing she'd ever imagined a male giving her times ten.

She forgot her mission and her entire existence. Nothing else mattered but having him inside her and sharing his incredible mind. She actually wailed with disappointment when he started to withdraw because she wanted the incredible sensations to go on forever.

She collapsed over him, her mouth pressed to the pulse of his throat as he smoothed his hands over her bare skin. Eventually, she remembered how to breathe and raised her head to find her partner staring up at the ceiling.

Guilt consumed her and she struggled to completely disengage herself from him.

"Gods I'm so sorry—I can't believe how I just behaved."

"It was the drugs. You weren't in control of your own body."

He sounded flat and...defeated, and that made it even worse.

"I— You didn't come."

He suddenly turned toward her, his golden gaze intent. "What is your first name?"

"It's Mya."

"I am Rekk. I think. You are from the Hakron tribe, yes?"

She nodded and then shivered when he ran his finger down her arm.

"Your skin is beautiful."

"Don't." She licked her lips. "Don't touch me. I'm still not completely in control of my body."

His smile was wry. "And you won't be for three days. That's the standard mating period for our kind isn't it?"

"I've never had a mating period. I'm in the military." She briefly closed her eyes. "Gods, I'm supposed to be finding a way to get us out of here, not thinking about fucking."

"There isn't a way out. I've tried everything."

His quiet acceptance shook her to the core.

"There *has* to be. There are two of us now. We can combine our abilities and—"

He placed his finger over her mouth. *"Don't talk. They are taping us."* She felt like an even bigger fool than before. *"If you wish to talk, do it while we're fucking. If we keep fucking, they won't interfere."*

"And what if we stop?"

He grimaced. *"More hormone shots for both of us."*

"But why? How is this even happening?"

He rolled on top of her, and her brain forgot about speech again as he angled his hips and slid back inside her. He was still hard.

"I can't think when we're doing this. Let alone plan an escape."

"You'll get used to it."

"Can't you ejaculate? That would buy us some recuperative time."

"No. They like to keep me hard."

She looked up into his golden eyes and saw nothing but resignation there. It was kind of humiliating that everything she was experiencing meant nothing to him. She reminded herself her feelings were an illusion, and that once she was out of her forced mating phase, she'd be as detached as he was.

But, for now, she couldn't stop surrendering to all the sensations. His rock-hard body and big cock, the amazing power of his mind as it meshed with hers when she climaxed. If it were all a dream, she would never forget it. He kept the tempo slower this time, allowing her to breathe and attempt to order her scattered thoughts.

"Can we try something?"

He didn't answer, but she took his silence as agreement.

"Can we use our combined power to break through the lock on this place?"

"It won't work."

"Have you ever tried it with another telepath?"

"No."

"Then can we just make an attempt?"

He sighed and slowed the thrust of his hips even more. *"If you wish."*

"I'll project if you could just add your power to mine?"

He lowered his head and sucked her nipple into his mouth, making her arch up against him and come around his cock in a series of slow, clenching bursts of excitement.

When she'd regained her breath, she focused on her second-in-command Roberts who was an unusual kind of telepath from planet Earth. If anyone could pick up her distress signal and get back to her it would be him.

"Now."

He added his power, and she almost blacked out as the force of it went through her and then rebounded. He tried to shield her as she writhed in shock.

"I told you it wouldn't work."

"We don't know that. Something could've gotten through," Mya replied. *"And even if it hasn't, I have another plan."*

MYA WAS DOZING on Rekk's chest, his cock still a stiff presence inside her. She had no idea how long she'd been locked up with him, but knew the longer they stayed, the more likely it was that whoever was in charge of the security unit would turn up. She had a strong sense that she didn't want to meet them.

Beneath her, Rekk stirred, his fingers combing through her hair.

"Mya?"

"Yes?"

"If we do attempt to escape and we are recaptured, there is something I would ask you to do for me."

Mya raised herself up on one elbow so that she could look into his beautiful golden eyes. There was nothing there to reassure her.

"What is it?"

She had a feeling she already knew the answer.

"Kill me. I'd rather die than end up back here." He traced the line of her jaw with his fingertip. *"I... cannot do this anymore. I've been trying to shut myself down over the past few months, but they insist on keeping me alive. I think that's why they captured you, to force me to keep living."* His mouth twisted. *"I'll go mad."*

"I understand."

"Then will you promise me?"

"Yes. If I can, I will make sure you aren't recaptured."

"Thank you." He slowly exhaled. *"And I will do the same for you."*

"Do you think they would try and keep me like this? And who exactly has the power to imprison you?"

"Aye, they would keep you. They'd rather have both of us, of course, but one telepath is enough to amuse an Etruscan or two." He shivered. *"They enjoy...dissecting me. They love my pain. I would not leave you alive to endure what I have suffered."*

"How did you get here?"

He frowned. *"I'm not sure. I think there was a crash and I was the only survivor. It was many years ago."*

Mya kissed his nose and switched into the spoken word. "Is there a bathroom?"

"Yes." His golden eyes looked puzzled at her abrupt change of subject.

"Can you take me there?"

"Of course." He hesitated. "You can go alone if you want to. There is no way out."

She forced a smile. "I'd rather you came with me. I'm frightened."

He raised an eyebrow. "If you wish."

He took her hand and walked with her to a concealed door at the back of the room, which slid open as they approached. *"There are cameras in here as well."*

She nodded as he went to wash his face and hands, leaving her free to pee. She finished up and turned toward him, her gaze fixed on his erect cock.

"I want you."

"Then come back to bed."

"No, here. Where I can watch you touch me in the mirror."

His pupils dilated until they were almost black and he reached for her, setting his hands around her waist, lifting her and bringing her feet flat on the countertop. She allowed her knees to fall open, giving him the perfect view of her sex in the mirror that hung over the washbasin.

"Touch me."

His cock was a hard rod against her spine and buttocks. He reached a hand around to play with her already sensitive clit and the slick folds of her sex, spreading her wide with his fingers until she moaned.

"Yes, just like that." she murmured, reaching back to brace her left hand on his massive biceps and placing her right palm flat on the wall.

"Help me. Put your hand over mine on the wall."

He complied, and she focused not on the pleasure, but on sucking out the plans for the power circuits controlling their prison. It was a useful telepathic skill she had learned from Major Esca's Female, Soreya. With Rekk's extraordinary telepathic abilities, it took just seconds.

Just as she was about to break off the connection, a faint voice registered in her mind.

"Captain. I have pinpointed your signal. Regret due to current political situation, cannot storm building. Team in position to help the moment you escape. Roberts over and out."

"Thank the Gods," Mya breathed as Rekk's fingers sank deep inside her and she climaxed, her whole body arching like a Hakron bow.

With a growl, Rekk picked her up turned her around to face him and dropped her down over his cock in one slick motion. Mya clung to him, her feet digging into the jut of his hips as he walked her back to the bed and fucked her hard. She took every thrust and gave it back to him until his smooth rhythm disappeared and he just rocked and held deep.

"I'm... going to come."

He sounded as desperate as she felt.

"Please..." She urged him on with her heel pounding into his buttock. *"Please."*

He increased his ragged pace, his breathing uneven as he drilled into her, making the whole bed rock.

"Not supposed to do this... haven't—Gods!"

The heat of him shocked her as he pumped her full of come and kept coming and thrusting until she forgot her own name and just joined him in a stream of consciousness that fused them together like two strands of melted wire. She didn't care whether this was real or not. Whatever happened, she would never forget how he'd made her feel.

"We'll have to leave soon."

Mya opened her eyes as he collapsed over her.

"Why?"

"Because I am not supposed to be able to do that. Mayhap they really do want us to procreate."

There was a grim note in his thoughts, which made Mya instantly revert into battle mode.

"Then let's do this." She focused on the plans she'd absorbed of the various power systems. *"I'll take out the power if you can work on the alarm systems and send any pursuit off in the wrong direction."*

Their minds were working in such perfect harmony that he immediately understood. He rolled off her, grabbed her hand and went toward the door.

"Let's go."

Mya took a deep breath, placed her hand on the wall beside the exit, and blasted everything she and Rekk had through the power circuit. Alarms started to blare as the door slid open to reveal Amar sitting half-asleep in a chair. Even as he struggled to his feet, Rekk was on him and Mya heard the crack of Amar's neck snapping. Rekk threw Amar's weapon to her, and she checked it over as they ran.

"Lead us away from the alarms, Rekk. All the doors are now unlocked except the outer security ones, which run on a more complex circuit. I'll have to get closer to make them open."

"Understood."

Ignoring the strident alarms, they sprinted down mostly deserted hallways, moving in a northerly direction away from the front of the building. As they ran, Mya kept reaching out to Roberts, hoping he'd be there as promised if things got rough.

"What the frek?" Kane stepped out of a doorway, his weapon half-raised. Mya didn't hesitate to shoot to kill. He dropped like a stone, blocking the passageway, but they jumped over him and kept moving.

"Approaching outside exit," Rekk said.

"Stand back, Captain Jong." Lieutenant Roberts's voice came through loud and clear.

Mya dragged Rekk to a halt as the exterior door blew inward, sending a cloud of debris toward them. Coughing and half-blinded by the smoke, she kept moving, pushing Rekk ahead of her and aiming all her energy toward the unique telepathic signal of Roberts.

"Five more meters up the slope, Captain. We've got you covered."

She put her head down and just slogged onward until she hit something solid. Roberts had already taken off his T-shirt and was shoving it down over her head.

"This is Rekk," she said breathlessly. "He's coming, too."

Roberts stared at the big man beside her and nodded. "Whatever you say. But let's go."

3

He didn't like the ship any more than he'd liked his Etruscan prison. They'd put him in "Medical," but it was just another name for a secure cage he couldn't escape. Rekk paced the small space, his mind in turmoil as the engines of the ship thrummed around him. The entire crew was telepathic, so thoughts were flying around like a rainstorm, making his head hurt.

Raising his fist, he punched the door hard enough to leave a dent. He obviously set off a silent alarm because moments later a white-coated female came through the door accompanied by the hard-faced man who had met them on the perimeter of his prison. This man's mind was *different*, his thoughts far less emotional than the typical telepath's, and his ability to block Rekk's power unexpected.

"My name is Lieutenant Roberts. I appreciate that you are disoriented and distressed, sir, but we are doing our best to get you back to Pavlovan as fast as possible."

"Where is the Female?"

"Are you referring to Captain Jong, sir?"

"Mya, aye." *My Female.*

"She is currently being processed by our medical staff."

"Get her."

"I will inform her that you wish to see her, sir," Roberts said.

"*Now*," Rekk growled, "or I will destroy this room and anyone who comes near me."

"If you refuse to cooperate, I will instruct the medical staff to knock you out for the duration of the journey."

Rekk bared his teeth at the medical tech who shrank behind Roberts. "If you touch me, I will kill you."

"If you touch her, *sir*, or anyone on this ship, I will fucking kill *you*. I don't care who you are. We rescued you. The least you can do is be grateful." Roberts's voice hardened. "There is no need for this. I will ask Captain Jong to come and see you when she is cleared by medical. Until then, I suggest you keep your temper."

He ushered the tech out of the room, leaving Rekk alone once more. With a groan, he sank down on the side of the bed.

Roberts was right. He was behaving like an animal driven by fear. He had no idea how long he'd been in that cell or how he had gotten there. All he knew was his name was Rekk. Or, at least he thought that was his name. Everything else came and went like a Pavlovan desert wind.

He took a deep steadying breath. These people were not his enemies. Mya had saved him, and he was going home. Home to an unknown future amongst a people who had obviously abandoned him.

MYA PUT on her uniform and studied her reflection in the mirror. Outwardly, she looked composed. Inwardly, she was still a mass of raging hormones who wanted to find her mate and fuck him. Yeah, that's what she'd been reduced to.

"Captain Jong?" The medic tapped on the door. "Lieutenant Roberts needs to speak to you urgently."

"I'm just coming."

Mya went out into the main room of the medical center where Roberts awaited her, his expression grim.

"What's the problem?" she asked, but she already knew from the horrendous pressure in her mind.

"Our guest is getting a little restless."

"I'm not surprised. He's been imprisoned in one room for years, and now we've stuck him in another one."

"Which he's currently threatening to destroy if he doesn't get to see you."

Mya winced. "Then I'll go and see him. How long until we get back to Pavlovan?"

"About four hours. I've been ordered to take us to Trenrick on the other side of the planet."

"The most secure base. That makes sense seeing as we're carrying an unknown entity on our ship. Did you manage to get a blood sample from him?"

"Yes and DNA. I haven't sent them. I assumed it might be better not to advertise our unexpected guest's presence on the open space channels."

"Good thought. We can hand them over when we land." Mya took a deep breath. "Can you make sure that all transmissions from medical are blocked?"

Roberts paused. "But what if he attempts to hurt you?"

"He won't."

Roberts inhaled. Did his enhanced senses mean he could tell that she was in a mating phase? "Are you quite sure you want to go in there, in your present physical state, Captain?"

"I don't think I have any choice." Mya straightened her spine. "If there is any problem, I promise I'll shout out."

Roberts reluctantly stepped aside, and she punched in the security code for the medical lab and went inside. Rekk sat on the bed, staring down at his clasped hands between his knees. He wore loose pants that Mya assumed were surgical scrubs and his chest was bare.

He slowly looked up. "He is a fool if he thinks I would hurt you."

"He's just being super careful."

Mya leaned back against the door as his scent reached her. Smelling him was like taking some mind-inducing drug that made her lose all her inhibitions. For someone who prided herself on being in control, even with her mate, it was frightening. She couldn't believe he was still affecting her like this. After giving her the counteragent, the medics had assured her the drugs were clear of her system.

But what if they were clear? There had to be more to this than just drugs. She couldn't pretend he hadn't come to mean something far more important to her than a forced mate. It wasn't uncommon in their culture for mates to instinctively recognize each other. The odds were low in a population the size of Pavlovan, but not impossible, which was why the Oracle was usually necessary to perform the introductions.

"*Are* you afraid of me?"

"No."

"Mayhap you should be." His golden stare measured her. "I am—"

"Stressed out." Mya finished for him. "Which is completely understandable, That's why I'm here."

"You intend to stand by the door the whole time?"

"I'm not sure if I should get any closer." She eyed his perfect chest. "I think I still want to have sex with you."

He palmed the already hard length of his shaft pushing against the thin fabric of his pants. "It seems I am primed to respond to you whether I wish to or not."

"Then I'll stay right here. I'll never take what isn't offered freely. You have my word. No one will ever force you again."

"Thank you." He paused. "The thing is. You are different. You, I want."

Her knees threatened to give way. "Don't say that."

Gods, she needed him to be the sane one—the one to push her away, and yet he seemed to feel the same way that she did.

He shrugged, which made his muscles ripple beneath his skin. "It is the truth. I cannot understand it myself."

"Which is another good reason why I should just stay over here. Everything is way too complicated at the moment for us to make it worse."

Her mind circled through possibilities. What was she supposed to do about Orin? She'd refused to go to the Temple to find their Third, and now she was starting to think that the male in front of her was that very person. Orin was hoping for a Second Female so he could finally have a child. How could she reconcile those two things without hurting someone? How could she remain true to herself?

He rose from the bed and came toward her, pressing one hand against the door behind her head. He was one of the very few men she had ever met who towered over her. With an inarticulate sound, he buried his face in the crook of her neck.

"I am afraid, Mya."

Her hand curved around the back of his neck. *"I know."*

He leaned into her, the hard ridge of his cock a hot brand against her stomach, and let her hold him.

"You will be fine."

A tremor ran through him and he nuzzled her skin, his teeth brushing her earlobe, making her shiver in return. *Fine* was such an inadequate thing to say when he was facing a completely uncertain future on a planet that had apparently abandoned him to his fate.

She gently pushed on his chest, and he took a faltering step backward, his hands fisted at his side.

"You are correct. We should not touch each other." Rekk said.

The thought of never touching him again—of losing her intimate sense of him overwhelmed her. She couldn't do it. She just couldn't.

She stripped off her uniform and regulation underwear.

"Mya…"

She guided him to the bed until he was sitting down and then knelt at his feet. This she could do for him. This she could offer him to help him survive. Orin would never criticize her for that. She pushed Rekk's knees wide, making a space for herself between them, and untied the drawstring of his pants. His hand covered hers.

"You do not need to do this."

"I want to."

He removed his hand and she worked the pants free until she could cup his balls and admire the long, hard length of his shaft. With a soft sound, she licked him from root to tip, making him jump. Pre-cum coated the crown of his cock, and she licked a slow, easy spiral around his slit, sipping at him, her tongue delving deep until his hand shoved into her hair to hold her.

"Mmm." The sound of her pleasure vibrated through him, and she closed her eyes and took more, sharing her explorations in her thoughts, showing him himself being slowly devoured.

"*Gods.*"

Seconds later, he picked her up and laid her on the bed, his broad shoulders spreading her thighs, his hands on her ass, lifting her up to his mouth. She was already wet for him, and he used his teeth and tongue to drive her to a climax.

With a growl, he lowered her onto his cock, sliding home in one smooth thrust as she continued to come. Her whole mind was engrossed with sensation and the sheer physicality of his body moving with hers. She wrapped her arms and legs around him and held him close, enveloping him in her mind as he gave himself up to the pleasure and to her.

"Mya."

She opened her eyes as he thrust one last time. His body went still as his come released hot and deep, setting her off into another orgasm as they came together.

It took her a long while to notice the lights had dimmed. An announcement was being sent over the comm—secondary power was being activated due to an unforeseen surge of telepathic energy through the system.

"I bet that was us," Mya murmured as she stroked Rekk's hair. "How embarrassing is that?"

But her lover wasn't listening; he was already moving again, his cock hardening with every shift of his hips. She gave herself up to desire. She was alive and so was he, and the space they currently shared was both limited and precarious. If her body gave him the ability to get through the next few hours without fear, she would offer it to him willingly.

After that she had no idea what to expect or what she intended to do.

***

It was late at night in his city precinct, and almost everyone else had gone home. The nightshift was out patrolling, which meant Orin had the place pretty much to himself. His colleagues were a nosy bunch, and he didn't particularly want them to know he'd lost track of his Female. He'd never hear the end of it. He stared at the comscreen and tapped his fingers impatiently against the desk.

"Put me through to Major Esca, then."

"Unable to comply."

Orin glared at the image as if it were real. "Then whom can I talk to about the nonappearance of my mate?"

The screen went blank and a male appeared, dressed in the uniform of the Special Forces. He had brown hair, pale blue eyes and an unremarkable face.

"Lieutenant Orin Mazra?"

"Yeah. Who are you?"

"I'm Lieutenant Roberts. I'm a member of Captain Jong's unit."

"Where the heeze is she?" Orin demanded. "She was supposed to be home yesterday."

"There was an incident during the operation that delayed our return, sir. Captain Jong is safe and well, but our ship has been redirected to Trenrick Base for security reasons."

"She isn't injured?"

"No, sir."

Orin almost sagged with relief. He couldn't take another death, especially the most important female in his world.

"Can I see her?"

"Negative, sir. Our entire crew is being held here for debriefing."

"Why?"

"As I mentioned, there was a classified incident that occurred off-planet."

"So, basically you won't tell me anything, and I can't see her."

"Exactly, sir."

"Why can't I speak to her on vid screen?"

"She's currently occupied, sir, and will be for some time as we follow landing procedures."

Orin rubbed a hand over the back of his neck. "Is she in trouble?"

"Not at all. If you wish me to give her a message, I can at least do that."

"Great." He sighed. "Tell her I love her and that I hope everything is all right."

Gods, that sounded so banal when his heart was thumping double-time and his gut was twisting with anxiety.

"Will do, sir." Roberts hesitated. "I wouldn't worry too much. She really is fine."

"Thanks. Over and out."

The screen went back to blue and Orin continued to stare at it. He didn't care what Roberts said. Something was wrong. If Mya was on-planet, he should sense her, but there was nothing. When he'd woken up that morning, he'd had a terrible sense that he was alone, and it had shocked him to the core.

Had he driven her away with his decision to tell her how bad he was feeling? Was she hiding herself from him and reluctant to come home? He couldn't put their last conversation out of his head, how defenseless she'd looked while he'd made all his high-handed demands, how frakking stupid he'd been to say anything in the first place...

He pushed away from the screen and returned to pacing the worn-out carpet. When she came back, he'd make sure she understood that what she wanted was just as important, if not more so, than what he wanted. He loved her. He'd shut her out. Not having her made him see that so clearly. She wasn't the only one who had taken their partnership for granted. He was just as guilty.

Orin took a deep breath. He could fix this. He had to.

MYA SHOWERED and scrambled into her uniform, emerging from her cabin just as the ship touched down at Trenrick military base. Roberts lined up alongside her as the main door was released.

"Message for you from Orin Mazra. He said to tell you he loved you, and that he hoped everything would be all right."

Mya winced. "He's going to kill me when he hears about all this."

"I doubt it. He sounded genuinely concerned about you."

"We're mated."

"Ah." Roberts looked anywhere but at her. "That will be an interesting conversation, although Pavlovans are free to have sex with anyone until a Triad decides to bond completely, right?"

"That's correct."

"Then seeing as you were forced into the situation, he can't really object."

"Are you trying to reassure me, Roberts?"

"I'm just trying to understand the complexity of Pavlovan mating. We don't tend to go in for telepathic threesomes on Earth."

"It's certainly a minefield." Intellectually, she was certain Orin would understand, but bonded males were often ruled by instinct, not intellect. "Who are we expecting to meet us here?"

The question was answered when Major Esca came through the door accompanied for four security guards.

"Captain Jong, Lieutenant Roberts." He saluted them. "Good to see you made it home."

"Thank you, sir."

"You okay, Jong?" His keen gaze searched her face.

"I'm fine, sir."

"Then take me to see this telepath."

Mya led the way. "He's understandably wary, sir."

"I'll be as non-threatening as I can." Major Esca paused. "Damn, I can feel his energy from here. He's right up there with Ash."

"Yes, sir."

Mya punched in the security code and led the major into the medical lab.

"Rekk, may I introduce Major Esca?"

"Major."

Rekk slowly stood up. He was of a similar height and weight to the other soldier, but their coloring was the complete opposite. The Major had black hair and blue eyes, and usually had a smile on his face, but not today. Rekk was making some effort to control his telepathic output, but being close to him was still like staring into the sun.

"I apologize." Rekk shrugged. "They experimented on my shields so that I could not hide my power from them. I will have to learn how to rebuild them."

Major Esca winced. "Yeah, otherwise we're all going to suffer. I'm used to Senator Ash's levels but—"

"Ash?" Rekk interrupted him. "Ash of the Skysan dynasty?"

"Yes. Do you know him?"

"I am not sure." Rekk frowned. "The name is familiar."

Major Esca nodded. "I regret that until we have verified who you are, performed some more medical tests, and asked you a million questions, we cannot allow you to leave this base."

"I understand."

Rekk turned to Mya who saluted him as well.

"My team will also be staying until we've been debriefed."

"This way, sir." Major Esca stepped to one side and indicated that Rekk should join him. "There is nothing to fear."

4

THE MEDICAL OFFICES AT THE BASE WERE DECORATED IN soothing shades of cream and green with inoffensive landscapes and inspirational quotes hung at regular intervals on the walls. In the waiting area there was usually soft music, which made Mya want to scream. Inside this *particular* room was a pink couch with lacy pillows that Mya had chosen not to sit on.

"I don't know." Mya darted a quick glance at the silent female opposite her. "I thought that by now I'd be back to normal, but I'm not. And it's not like me. I'm generally organized, focused, and fully committed to the advancement of my military career."

"What do you think the problem is, Captain?"

Mya lifted her head. She hated all this psychological shit. Perhaps it was time to stop skirting around and get to the heart of the issue that was bothering her and to hell with their reactions.

"Is it possible that I bonded with Rekk?"

"Well, you certainly had sexual relations with him. What makes you think there was any more to it? You were drugged against your will and forced to copulate whether you wanted to or not. That hardly seems like the basis for a consenting relationship."

"I am aware of that." Mya hung on to her patience. "Which is precisely my point because despite everything, I can't seem to extricate myself from his mind."

The therapist leaned forward, her hands clasped together in her lap. "His shields have been compromised. He might be finding it difficult to shut off your previous connection."

"I know that. So, can I just… talk to him face to face, and see if we can find a way to sort it out?"

She hadn't seen Rekk for three days, but she knew exactly how he was feeling because she couldn't shut down their damned link. From the moment they'd entered the base, the whole team had been separated, interviewed, and medically examined until Mya was ready to scream. If she had to tell one more person her version of what had happened, she would turn into a babbling idiot.

"Do you think that would be a good idea?" the therapist asked gently. "If you see him, it might increase your attraction to him. It is possible that you believe you are mated to him because you feel guilty about enjoying your sexual encounter."

"Or it might prove I am mistaken. Between us, we might be able to shut this thing down."

"You believe he is responding to you?"

There was a note of disbelief in Dr. Lyn's voice that put Mya instantly on the defensive.

"And why would that be a problem? Is it because I'm Hakron?" Mya asked. "Is there any reason why he *couldn't* be our Third?"

She couldn't actually believe she was asking the question because the whole idea of finding another bonded mate and forming a Triad was a minefield for her.

Dr. Lyn rose from her seat. "I think it's time you talked to Major Esca and my boss. Come with me."

Mya followed her into a different part of the medical complex and endured the unusually high security checks, both physical and mental, before she was allowed into yet another large office with comfortable chairs that looked out of place on a military base.

A man came to greet her, his hand held out. He wore the formal white garb she normally associated with members of the Senate.

"Captain Jong? I'm Dr. Frith. It's a pleasure. Please come and sit down."

He ushered her into a chair opposite Major Esca, who was looking rather conflicted.

"Jong."

"Major."

Dr. Frith cleared his throat. "Dr. Lyn tells me that during your mandated sessions with her you have been struggling with your telepathic connection to the male you know as Rekk."

"I wouldn't say I was *struggling* with it, sir. I just don't seem to be able to shut him out."

"Which has made you wonder whether you are actually mated to him, correct?"

Mya heard both sympathy and condescension in his tone and stiffened. "I wish to understand why the connection still exists. Obviously, I would need to consult with my current mate to see if we both recognized Rekk as our Third."

Gods, there she went again talking her mouth off as if finding a Third was something she'd always wanted.

Major Esca sat forward. "Jong, what we are about to discuss is confidential and not to be repeated outside this room, okay?"

"Yes, sir."

Dr. Frith consulted his notes. "We extracted DNA, blood, and did all the other necessary tests on our guest and the results were... unexpected. There were also other abnormalities. Whoever was holding him on that Etruscan moon interfered with his ability to shield and tampered with his nervous system. That collar and the metal shackles he wore all contained probes that constantly monitored his every physical and telepathic response."

"He said they were experimenting on him and enjoyed causing him pain," Mya said. "He also said that he was visually monitored day and night."

"We should be able to help him restore his shields and improve his nervous system, but it will take time." Dr. Frith hesitated. "More worrying is his loss of memory and his sense of alienation from his own people."

Mya shifted in her seat. "Don't you think he has a perfect right to be angry about being abandoned like that? I still can't believe it happened to him. If he was military, how come no one went back for him?"

"Why do you assume he was military?"

"Why else would he be in space?" Mya glanced at Major Esca and then at the doctor. "What am I missing?"

"We think," Dr. Firth said carefully. "That Rekk's bloodline and telepathic abilities come from the Pavan dynasty."

"One of the families that originally settled this planet? Didn't they all die out centuries ago?" Mya desperately tried to remember her history. "That doesn't make sense."

"We also think he's about one hundred and twenty-five years old."

"Wow." Mya just about remembered how to shut her mouth. "That's not possible."

"The Oracle is older, and the last surviving member of the Pavan dynasty died at almost two hundred years."

"How do you know Rekk is Pavan?"

"Because some of his ancestors left their blood samples in our memory banks, and we also have some more distant relatives like our own Senator Ash who share some similar genetic traits."

"So Rekk is kind of an anomaly. Have you told him?"

"No. In our opinion, he isn't ready to receive the information yet. We are currently focusing on detaching him from the collar and cuffs and boosting his immune system to cope with the current climate."

Mya tensed. "Did he agree to you doing those things to him? The last time I saw him, he was rather anti-scientist."

For the first time Dr. Frith looked slightly uncomfortable. "He was… resistant to any interventions."

Mya held her breath. "You put him under, didn't you? I wondered what was going on today. I thought that maybe he'd broken the connection after all, but it hasn't gone away completely." She shook her head. "He's going to freak out when he comes around. Don't you think you might have waited until he was more stable to start messing with him again?"

Major Esca shook his head. "We needed to get the Etruscan probes out of his system as fast as possible. We cannot have their spy systems tracing him here."

"I should imagine the Etruscan government knows exactly where he is already."

"No, that's the weird thing, Jong. We have heard nothing official about his loss at all."

Mya frowned. "The guard I met there said we were off the grid and that no one would know what had happened to me. The whole place was shielded from telepathic thoughts. It was only because Lieutenant Roberts works on a different frequency that I was able to get through to him." Mya leapt to her feet and started pacing. "Maybe the Etruscan government doesn't know what was going on in there, either."

"You might be right, but we still had to get rid of those probes. It might help restart his memory as well." Major Esca glanced at Dr. Firth. "We were intending to ask you to remain as Rekk's primary contact, but I gather from what Dr. Lyn is telling us that this might be a problem?"

For a second Mya hesitated. She *must* have imagined there was a connection between her and Rekk. He was from the premier family of the planet, whereas she was from a small Hakron village buried in Quoxor Province. She'd only been given a chance in the military because her father had been one of the Oracle's Temple bodyguards. There was no chance in hell that they were mated. She should be relieved, but she wasn't feeling it yet.

"I don't think there will be a problem, sir."

Dr. Lyn leaned forward. "With all due respect, Captain, I think your… *attachment* to Rekk might cause all kinds of problems for both of you."

"But we don't have a choice, do we?" Mya focused on Dr. Frith, knowing Major Esca would give her his backing regardless. "Perhaps when Rekk recovers from his surgery, his shields will have reset automatically and there won't be a problem. I won't know until I see him. And if you don't let me work with him, I suspect he might get agitated like he did on the ship home."

"Yes, Roberts told me about that," Major Esca said. "He also said that Rekk's power level dropped significantly when you were with him acting as a shield and anchor."

"Then let me at least talk to him," Mya offered. "If I find it too difficult, I'll walk away and get Roberts to handle him or something."

Dr. Lyn frowned. "Perhaps you should get Lieutenant Roberts to perform this duty anyway."

"I wish I could, but Rekk has specifically asked for Captain Jong. " Major Esca stood up. "We need to get Rekk to see the Oracle. She is the only person who can truly verify if he is who we think he is."

"Then you wish me to accompany him to the Temple? I can do that. It isn't far."

"We can't fly him down there. Number one, he's not going to

be willing to be put back on a plane, and two, last time we sent a Senate-registered flyer down there, it was attacked by the Etruscans and I nearly lost my mate." Major Esca's expression was grim. "So this journey will have to be in civilian clothes and in civilian transportation. An undercover operation. Just a couple going to visit the Oracle at the Temple to find out who their Third is."

Mya immediately thought of Orin. "Can I share any of this with my bonded mate?"

"No, I'm sorry, Jong."

"Can I at least ask him to meet me at the Temple? We were supposed to be going there after this mission to find our Third anyway." Mya hesitated. "I *promised* him."

"Okay, I know he is worried about you—he's been calling every damned day, so meet him at the Temple if he wants that."

"Thank you, sir."

"But don't tell him a thing about Rekk or how you are going to get to the Temple. I don't want any mistakes."

"Understood, sir." Mya saluted and then looked over at Dr. Frith. "I'll contact Orin, and then I'll be ready to see Rekk when he awakens from the surgery."

<hr>

"Mya, thank the *Gods* you are all right."

She studied Orin's drawn features on the vidscreen as tears rose in her throat. He looked so safe, so darling, and so familiar. After the last week of dealing with Rekk and the overwhelming force of his abilities, the reality of Orin was just what she needed.

"When are you coming home? I'll get leave. Don't worry about that—I'll do whatever it takes—"

She pressed her fingers against the curve of his jaw on the screen. "I... can't come back yet."

His expression stilled. "What's wrong? Are you hurt? Or in trouble, or—"

"I can't tell you anything except that I'm fine, and I'm still involved in this mission."

He stared at her so intently he might as well have been in the room with her. "What's wrong?"

"There's nothing wrong."

"I don't believe you." He shoved a hand through his short, dark hair. "Look, if this has got anything to do with all that shit I dumped on you just before you left? Then forget it all. I was an idiot. The most important thing I have in my life is you, and I'm not going to fuck that up."

Mya found herself smiling at him. Unlike her, he'd never been the kind of person to hold back his thoughts. "It's okay. I've been doing a lot of thinking as well. I can't be with you right now, but I'd like to meet you at the Temple in Quoxor Province when I've completed my mission."

If she could contemplate having Rekk as a Third, she couldn't deny Orin the chance either. Sometimes in life one had to take a leap of faith, and Orin deserved everything she had.

"At the Temple?" He blinked at her, his voice unsteady. "Mya, love, you don't have to do that. I'm not going to force you to do anything you aren't ready for."

"I want to try. I can't let my past hold me back for the rest of my life. Do you think you can get leave to do that?"

"To meet at the Temple? Yeah. I think that's mandatory if you are looking for a bonded mate." He blew out his breath. "Mya—that's just amazing of you."

"I'm not sure exactly when I'll get there, but I'd reckon about a week from now."

He nodded. "That's fine. I know you won't be able to keep in touch while you're working, but let me know when you're close to getting there, and I'll take the first flight out. I promise."

She blew him a kiss, her fingers unsteady. "I love you, Orin. I'll tell you everything I can when I see you, okay?"

"I'm counting on it. I love you, Mya."

"You, too, Orin."

His face faded to be replaced by a blue screen and military logo. Damn. She still felt horrible concealing the rest of it from him, but some things needed to be discussed in person, and what had happened between her and Rekk definitely qualified as one of them.

Would Orin understand? Mya hoped he would understand better than she did herself. Unlike Major Esca, she didn't belong to an exclusive mated Triad who only bedded each other. She only had Orin, and had deliberately kept it that way, so her liaison with Rekk shouldn't bother anyone. Except it bothered her, and if she was affected by it, Orin would be, too.

But what if Rekk *was* their Third?

She pushed that thought away. He was an anomaly. A male out of his own time and with a telepathic power almost never seen anymore. How could she even *consider* he might belong to her and Orin? Major Esca was probably right that she simply proved to be a good anchor to Rekk's shattered shields. And if that was what he needed from her—she would do her best to give it to him.

OPENING ONE CAUTIOUS EYE, Rekk forced himself to acknowledge that he had woken up in another sterile white room with machines attached to him. He fought to stop screaming. He wasn't back with the Etruscans, and whatever his current physicians had done to him hadn't left him in more pain than he'd been in before. Both of those things were good.

He still hated it, though.

"Rekk?"

He opened his other eye as his Female came out of a chair beside his bed and peered down at him. She was a tall, queenly woman. Her black hair was unbound and lay around her shoulders, framing the perfection of her face. He wished she was curled up beside him on the bed again.

"Mya."

Her smile was sleepy. "You okay in there?" She put her hand on his bare arm, the green contrasting with his more golden tones. "Don't panic or anything. They've been taking your collar and cuffs off and extracting all the probes embedded in your skin and nervous system."

"That is good."

"Yes."

He carefully put his hand over hers. "You will stay?"

"If you want me to." She indicated the chair beside the bed. "It's quite comfortable, actually."

She wore a soft blue shirt and pants that reminded him of a much less formal version of her uniform. Of course, he'd seen her naked, which was even more pleasing to his eye.

Her shields slammed into place, making him jump, and she carefully eased her hand away from him.

"Do you want something to eat or drink? I'll go check in with the medical staff as to what you're allowed."

"Mya."

She was already turning away from him.

"Yeah?"

"I did not mean to embarrass you."

"You didn't." She flashed him a quick smile. "Let me just go and fetch your nurse."

He frowned as she went out. What had changed? Had the loss of his Etruscan shackles altered his telepathic abilities as well? Mayhap it was for the best. He had no idea who he was, and he was hardly a fit mate for a fine upstanding Female like Captain Jong. He'd been little more than a prostitute chained to a bed and forced to perform any sexual act demanded of him. No wonder she didn't even want to look at him.

"She's coming to check you over." Mya came back to his side and picked up his cup. "Would you like some of this? I'll put some fresh ice in it if you like."

"You do not have to stay."

She paused, her hand reaching out to the jug. "I thought you—"

"I am sure you have more important duties to perform than to waste your time on me."

"Rekk..." She put down the cup. "I'd like to stay, but if you don't want me here all you have to do is say so. I thought having someone you know around would be helpful, but maybe it's just me. Would you prefer Lieutenant Roberts?"

"The frosty-eyed male who is like no telepath I have ever encountered before?" Rekk shuddered. "No, thank you."

"Then I'll stay."

The nurse came in and Rekk was poked and prodded and eventually allowed to sit up with the promise of a late supper if he was feeling like it.

"Do you feel any different?" Mya put down the flat screen she was reading from. "Dr. Frith said they took a lot of Etruscan hardware out of you."

"I certainly feel changed. Some of the memories that I hid from the Etruscans are starting to re-emerge into the light. " He fingered the sheet. "Do you still sense me or have I faded away?"

She made a face. "I was kind of hoping you would fade away, but—"

"You wish me gone?"

"I wish you to get well, to rebuild your shields and be happy." She met his gaze, her brown eyes steady.

"I will do my best, Mya."

"I know this is difficult for both of us, and I'm sure you want to forget what happened as much as I do."

"How can I regret it when I am now a free man?"

"I'm glad you are free and that I was there to help you. I meant more that you don't have to worry about all the other stuff that happened."

"You mean our mating?"

Her skin blushed a darker green on her cheeks. "Our forced mating. We both had no choice."

She obviously did regret consorting with him, and who could blame her? He slowly inclined his head. "I have no intention of embarrassing you, Captain Jong."

"That's not what I meant—"

"It is all right. I understand. We will keep our shields in place and behave like two civilized individuals. I am quite capable of doing that, you know."

"I would never think otherwise." She cleared her throat. "Which is good because the authorities have asked me to accompany you to the Temple at Quoxor."

"To see the Oracle? I remember her. What an excellent idea. If anyone can help unravel the mystery of who I am it will be her."

"There have been a series of Etruscan attacks on the Temple and on government ministers, so I've been asked to take you incognito."

"As I'm unsure of who I am anyway, that should not present a problem, but what exactly do you mean?"

"We'll travel to the Temple as a private couple seeking our Third. There will be additional security measures in place around us at all times, but for all intents and purposes, it will appear as if we are all alone."

"I understand." Rekk sank back against his pillows, suddenly aware of how vulnerable his neck felt without the weight of the golden collar. When had he come to accept his shackles as a normal part of him? How long had he been held in captivity and grown used to being at the Etruscan's mercy?

"Rekk, are you okay?"

He opened his eyes to see that Mya was standing by the bed, her expression full of concern. He forced himself to calm down.

"I am just tired. I think I will sleep now."

She gently touched his hand. "Go ahead. I'll be here when you wake up, I promise."

5

Rekk examined the clothing someone had laid out for him on the bed. Since the removal of the Etruscan probes, flashes of his past that he'd buried deep inside his mind had begun to emerge into the light. When he'd last been on Pavlovan soil, men had worn long tunics with elaborate sashes in soft silks and bright fabrics.

"What is this?" He held up the top item.

Mya wandered over to his side. "The blue fabric? The fashion came from planet Earth. They are called jeans."

He poked the stiff leggings and studied them. "The material is rough."

"But very hardwearing."

"Why would that matter? It is not as if I am destined to work in the fields."

Her smile dimmed. "Lucky you. Most of us like jeans because they last for a long time and are very comfortable. They will also provide excellent camouflage as almost everyone wears them."

"Ah." He had erred in some way. "What does one wear with them?"

She surveyed the pile of clothes. "Socks, boots, and a T-shirt for starters, and maybe a jacket or a hoodie."

He stripped off his hospital garb and reached for the jeans. "I shall try them."

Her gaze dropped to his groin. "Um, underwear, boxers, something to shield your... softer parts from the zipper of the jeans."

Of course now that she was staring at him nothing was remaining soft.

She handed him a pair of shorts. "These. Put these on first."

He drew the underclothing up his legs and attempted to arrange his now hard cock within the clinging fabric. She must think him a whore to be aroused so easily by a female's gaze. He pressed a hand to cover the curve of his balls and rigid cock.

"I apologize."

"It's not your fault. It's just those hormones. I was the one who was staring." Mya was looking everywhere but at him, her cheeks flushing.

He grabbed the jeans out of her lax grip. "Mayhap you could find me something to wear over the jeans while I put them on?"

"Sure."

She turned away and he struggled to step into the jeans and draw them up his legs. His breath hissed out as he caught the underside of his balls with the rough inner seam.

"Are you okay?" Mya asked. "The best way to put them on without catching anything important is to protect yourself with one hand inside the zipper."

"Ah." Rekk jiggled the metal fastening. "I do not understand how this works."

"Would you like me to show you?"

Rekk briefly closed his eyes. He'd like her to put her hand on his cock and keep it there until her fingers were covered with his come, but he had a feeling that wasn't what she wanted to hear.

"Let me." She made a soft, breathy noise as she reached around him, cupped his covered cock and balls with one hand and drew the metal tag upward, meshing the metal teeth together like a train track. "See? Right to the top and then you take out your hand and fasten the button."

He almost groaned when she removed her hand. He could smell his pre-cum on her fingers and his cock was throbbing in time to his heartbeat.

"Thank you." He turned away from her and clothed himself in the first shirt he saw. "Now all I need are some shoes."

"Okay."

From the corner of his eye he saw her bring her palm to her mouth and inhale. Was that the hand she had shoved down his pants? Why would she be doing that if she wasn't—

"I'll go and check on our travel documents, okay? Why don't you finish dressing and then pack the rest of the stuff in your bag?"

She practically ran to get away from him, which was even more bewildering. He packed his bag and then sat on the bed. He hoped to the Gods she would return. He wanted to get to the Oracle's Temple and find out who he was and his place in this new and frightening world.

***

"Oh Gods, oh Gods..." Mya ran into her bathroom, locked the door, and stripped off her clothes, her fingers pressed hard to her mouth as she inhaled the luscious, panty-melting scent of Rekk's cock.

Within a second, she had those same fingers pressed deep inside her and then she was coming hard, her breathing ragged and her body convulsing deep inside as she rocked back and forth on her knees.

"Gods..." She collapsed on the bath mat, her head in her

hands. Why had she volunteered for this mission again? One glimpse of his naked body and one touch of his cock had turned her into a raging, demanding sex fiend again. He was a vulnerable man in an impossible situation. She had to give him his dignity, and climbing on top of him and fucking him until they both screamed was not on the agenda.

And he'd made it very clear that, although his body was still responding to hers, his mind and his emotions were not. She had to respect that. With a deep sigh, she washed up, packed her bag, and made her way back to Rekk's room. The travel permits had been delivered earlier, and now there was nothing to stop them beginning their journey out of the city.

"IF YOU ARE WEARY, Mya, please consider resting your head on my shoulder," Rekk said softly. "I will not let you fall." And holding her while she slept would give him a tiny taste of the comfort he was denying himself.

They were on some kind of public transport system that was taking them on the first leg of their journey into Quoxor Province. The carriage was full and the atmosphere light as people either commuted home or were leaving the confines of the city behind.

"Are you sure?" Her brown eyes met his. "I don't want to be a pain."

"You are not. I am happy to be of service."

She angled her face against his shoulder and gave a deep, shuddering sigh. "I'm still a bit out of sorts since our last mission."

"Then sleep. I will watch over you and keep you safe."

Even as he said the words, he wondered if they were true. He was the hunted one here, and she was protecting him. There were supposedly other security personnel on the transport with them, but he hadn't detected anything unusual. To be fair, he was more worried about sensing the unique signal of an Etruscan telepath, which might indicate that his old captors were after him again.

He tried to relax and reminded himself that the removal of his collar and shackles should have destroyed any link between him and the Etruscans. But he was still wary. One thing he knew was that if they tried to take him back, he would die rather than submit to experimentation again. He had no memory of how he had been captured in the first place, which wasn't reassuring when he had thought of himself as a warrior.

This world... He glanced outside again. It was nothing like he remembered it. How much time had passed since he'd been captured? He couldn't sense anyone except Mya, but that might be because of the damage inflicted on his shields and telepathic abilities. It didn't have to mean he was alone.

A tiny snore escaped Mya and he smiled down at her. Her hand came to rest on his chest and she softened against him until there was no space between their bodies where they touched. Rekk's cock kicked up and he mentally groaned. Mya might have a more comfortable journey, but it seemed that he was destined to suffer. The jeans she had told him to wear made no allowances for the growth of his shaft and pinched in many places. He couldn't wait until he could strip naked again.

He focused his thoughts on reconstructing the fragile barriers of his mind. Too many people stopped to stare at him as if caught by the strength of his thoughts, and that was not a good way to remain anonymous. As he painstakingly rebuilt the connections, he watched the outside world go by, marveling at the changes on his planet, and became increasingly convinced that he'd been away for far longer than he'd realized.

Was any of his family still alive? Surely if they still lived they would've sought him out at the military hospital or at least been informed of his return.

Mya was all he had—an anchor in a sea of uncertainty. His feelings for her were unexpected and inconvenient. In captivity he'd trained himself not to react to anything or anybody. But one night with Mya had destroyed all that and left him unsure of how to proceed. When he'd last been on Pavlovan, if he'd been interested in a female he would simply have expressed that desire, and it would've been instantly fulfilled.

He already had the sense to realize that the world didn't work like that anymore, and that the females he'd recently encountered were valued alongside the men. But where did that leave him?

"Next stop Paloma."

The bus driver's loud announcement woke Mya from her doze, and she sat bolt upright and rubbed at her eyes,

"That's our first stop."

Rekk reached for her hand. "Then I'll retrieve our bags."

THE ROOM WAS small with a single window and a bathroom that barely had space for a tiny shower, a toilet, and a sink.

Mya grimaced as she put her bag on the bed they were going to have to share. There was a big festival in Paloma and lodgings had apparently been hard to find.

"You'd think the government would spend a bit more money on us than this dump. But I can't say I'm surprised. We'll have to find somewhere to eat because there isn't a restaurant in the hotel."

"It will suffice." Rekk placed his bag on the chair and stretched his arms over his head. "Gods, I am cramped from sitting in one space for so many hours."

His T-shirt rose to expose his toned abs and Mya hastily turned away. He looked damn fine in his street clothes, but she already knew he looked even better underneath. A male with a body like a sculpture should wear as few clothes as possible. And there she went again, panting over a man who had told her in no uncertain terms that he wasn't available.

"I'll just use the bathroom and then we can go out for a walk, okay?" She darted past him and closed the flimsy door. She didn't think she could stand being in that small room with him for hours. His scent drove her mad. How she was going to get to sleep lying that close to him was something she refused to think about.

After she finished in the bathroom, Rekk took his turn while she unpacked her bag, pulled on shorts and a T-shirt, and slipped her feet into a pair of sandals. The room was already too hot and she doubted there would be much air conditioning.

"Mya."

She looked up to find Rekk in his boxers in the doorway, his body dripping with water, and she forgot how to breathe.

"What should I wear now?"

She tried not to drool. "Shorts would work."

"Do I have some?"

She rummaged in his bag and found him a change of clothes. "Here you go."

"Thank you." He hesitated. "I find this manner of dress somewhat confusing."

"Why, what did you wear back in your day?"

His smile was sweet. "Silken robes, skin…"

She pictured him like that, imagined pushing the robe off his shoulders and kissing each piece of flesh it revealed.

His fingers clenched on the clothes she had given him.

"Sorry," she blurted out. "I'm trying, I really am."

He nodded and turned away from her. "I will be as quick as I can."

WITHIN MINUTES, they were walking out onto the busy street. Paloma was a well-known stop on the way to the Temple complex at Quoxor and was filled with hotels and restaurants to cater to the passing trade.

Mya glanced up at Rekk, who was looking rather fierce and attracting way too much attention.

"Can you raise your shields?" she asked quietly.

"I am trying, but all these telepaths are distracting me."

She took his hand. "How about I help?"

"If you wish. I will try not to embarrass you."

"It's not a problem. I just don't want the Etruscans to find you again." She focused inward and sent her energy toward him. Her mind blended smoothly with his, surrounding her with his special blend of heat and light. It seemed such a shame to have to mute his talents, but in their present situation it was essential.

"What do you like to eat?" Mya asked. "They have food from every region of the planet here. Where did you grow up?"

"I'm not sure. I remember it was hot—hence the lack of clothing." His smile was disarming.

"I was born quite near the Temple myself," Mya offered. "My father was one of the Oracle's bodyguards."

"A very honorable position. You did not choose to join him there?"

"I... moved away when I was five. My mother formed a new Triad."

"Your father died young, then?"

"Yes, in the Oracle's service. That's why I was eventually able to get away— I mean, join the military."

He kept hold of her hand as they crossed the busy street. "It is still an unusual choice for a Hakron, yes?"

"Yeah." She sighed. "Especially a female. I had to work about ten times as hard to convince my instructors that I had the necessary grit to succeed. They thought I would be too placid."

"Then they did not know you very well. You have the heart of a true fighter."

"Thank you. I'm about to be the first Hakron female to reach the rank of Major in the Pavlovan Special Forces."

"Impressive." He paused and inhaled. "Something smells good over there."

She looked at the restaurant in front of them. "Quoxor food, which is fine by me. Let's go in."

He hesitated. "I have no… funds."

"That's okay. I have credits from the military for this journey. As long as we don't have a ten-course banquet, I think we'll be fine."

ORIN COULDN'T SETTLE. On an impulse, he'd started his journey to Quoxor earlier than needed, taking advantage of accumulated leave and the obligatory days for any Pavlovan seeking a mate at the Temple. He'd decided to take his time, enjoy the journey, and maybe get some peace and perspective at the sacred site before Mya joined him.

Except he wasn't feeling peaceful. He was about halfway to Quoxor and Mya's telepathic signal kept flaring up in his head. She wasn't her usual self, and she wasn't attempting to contact him. She was just *there*—a constant nagging in his brain, pulsing with unknown energy that kept breaking through her regular shields and making itself at home in Orin's head.

The foreign energy attached to hers both fascinated and repelled him. It was definitely male. Orin tried to think of scenarios for what was happening with his mate, but could come up with nothing that made any sense. Had she been more severely injured on the mission than he'd been told? Was some shrink in her head trying to fix stuff?

He was worried and the constant headache wasn't helping.

He'd dumped his bag at a cheap hotel and gone out looking for a bar and something to eat. Maybe he could drown some of his worries that way. Orin paused as two men pushed past him, his trained cop senses immediately activated by their body language and the dense solidity of their shields.

Whatever the men were up to wasn't good. Glad to have something to do other than wallow in a bar, he decided to follow them. As he walked, he checked in with the local law-enforcement channels, but all was quiet except for the usual background chatter.

They were now entering the town square, which was where most of the restaurants and cafes were situated to catch the pilgrims and tourists. Even as he quickened his pace, a large black vehicle turned the corner, blocking the square's furthest exit, and another came in just behind him, blocking the rear.

The men were now running toward a small eatery on the left side of the square. A surge of adrenalin spiked in Orin's mind as one of the two threw something that shattered the window of the restaurant, spreading smoke and confusion. He blinked against the sudden flare and flung up his hand.

"Mya?"

Someone started screaming and tourists ran from the smoke. Orin ripped off his jacket and went forward automatically, transmitting what was happening to the local police corps. They might not be there yet—but he was.

"GET DOWN!"

Mya grabbed hold of Rekk and shoved him as hard as she could to the floor as something smashed through the glass and went off with a roar and a blinding flash.

Rekk rolled with her, covering her body with his own.

"Keep down and head toward the rear entrance. It's just to our left. Expect someone to be waiting for us outside."

Mya found her weapon, and, using a secure telepathic channel to the other security guards, relayed their position and her plan. There was no answer, which wasn't encouraging.

She went ahead of Rekk, crawling on hands and knees through the choking smoke. At the last moment, she ignored the back entrance and veered left through the tiny kitchen. The small staff had already bolted and something was scorching on the stove. She reached up to turn off the burner as she passed. There was no need to destroy the place completely.

A flare of aggression shot through her senses, and she paused to consider their options. It was highly likely someone was watching the kitchen exit as well. She tapped Rekk's arm and motioned toward the trap door set in the floor. He nodded and opened it easily, revealing a line of stone steps and some basic lighting.

She went past him, scanning for Etruscan signals as she went down the steps into the cellar. The space contained several refrigeration units and shelving for produce. There was also, thank the Gods, an exit.

The thud of the door closing over their heads deadened the alarms sounding from above as Rekk came down the steps to join her.

"Are you okay?" She touched his shoulder, where a bruise was already darkening the flesh under the ripped sleeve of his T-shirt.

"I am well." He touched her forehead with one finger. "You, however, are bleeding."

She tried to shrug it off. "It doesn't hurt."

"But we should tend to the wound."

"There's a medical kit on the shelf over there. It's the box with the yellow cross on it." She slowly exhaled. "But we don't have time. We need to get out of here."

"With you all bloodied? Surely that will draw the wrong kind of attention onto us? The immediate threat has passed; can you not feel it?" He retrieved the medical supplies. "When you are cleaned up, we can borrow a couple of the restaurant T-shirts and exit when we are ready."

His calm manner was both reassuring and surprising. She cupped his chin, where a fine fuzz of beard was forming, and rubbed the pad of her thumb against the bristles.

"Okay."

His breath hitched and he lowered his mouth to hers in a brief kiss. "Yes. Now let me attend to your face, and we can be on our way."

ORIN SURVEYED the destroyed front of the restaurant. The sirens were still shrieking, and there was glass everywhere that glinted in the lights of the approaching emergency vehicles. He tried to control his breathing. If Mya *had* been in there, she had either died or gotten away because he was getting no sense of her now.

Gods, she couldn't be dead. He'd know—wouldn't he?

A shadow fell over him and he turned around only to have a weapon jammed against his throat.

"You are under arrest."

"I'm a frakking cop. I called this in."

The male officer didn't bother to reply as he restrained Orin's wrists behind him. He knew better than to struggle, as the plastic would only tighten up.

"Come on, sir."

With one last searing glance at the destroyed restaurant, Orin allowed himself to be taken away. Once he sorted things out with the local police force, he'd gain access to all the information they had on the attack and what was really going on. At least, he hoped he would. And if Mya was involved? He'd find that out as well.

MYA PULLED the restaurant T-shirt over her head. "Right, I'm ready to go."

Rekk had changed as well and added some kind of cap to cover his golden hair, which was an excellent idea.

"Which exit do you wish to use? The one here or shall we chance our luck upstairs?"

Mya considered their options. "Let's go with this one. From what I can tell, it links up with other shops in the square, so we could come out further along the row and look even less suspicious."

"Then let's go."

When they finally gained the upper level of the square, Mya couldn't resist a quick glance over her shoulder. The whole front of the restaurant where they'd been sitting was gone, and the entire square was filled with emergency vehicles and flashing lights.

Rekk grabbed her hand. "Come on."

To her surprise, they were back at their hotel before she had time to breathe. He pulled her inside, locked the door, and then stood there crushing her, his whole body shuddering against hers.

"Gods..."

She looped her arms around his neck and just held on as his mouth descended on hers in a rough, demanding kiss. She shoved a hand up the back of his T-shirt and climbed him until her core was rubbing against the stiff rod of his cock. With a stifled sound, he pushed his shorts down, freeing himself before dealing with her clothes, baring the important parts so that he could lift her down over him in one swift motion, making them both groan.

Mya kept her eyes open as they fucked. She knew everything would be hurting later, but this wasn't about then, it was about celebrating survival in the most basic way possible. He hitched her even higher and drove deeper, making her cry out his name and climax, squeezing his thick length as he pounded into her.

For the first time in her life she wanted to forget being cautious and just live in the moment. This gorgeous man belonged with her and Orin—she knew it in her soul.

He came hard, impaling her against the door with the force of his final thrust, and she let it wash over her in rippling waves that consumed her. And that wasn't all. She returned every sensation to him until their thoughts were wrapped up so tight, there was no longer any distance between them.

With a ragged sound, he walked her over to the bed and fell backward onto it. The moment he hit the thin covers, she started undressing him completely, and he reciprocated, ripping her shorts in his haste to get her as naked as he was. She straddled him, her breasts bouncing. He leaned forward to lick and play with her curves until he set his teeth gently on her nipple and she moaned.

"Gods... Rekk, I want you... I want everything."

"Then take me. I am yours."

She wrapped one hand around his already rejuvenated cock and slowly lowered herself onto his hard, throbbing flesh, sharing every sensation with her hands, her mind, and her spirit. He sucked in a breath as she settled over him, one hand coming to rest on the curve of her hip.

"You are...different."

She stared down into his golden eyes. "You think?"

"I *know.*" He hesitated, his breath hitching as she used her internal muscles to squeeze the length of his cock. "You are not holding anything back."

She dropped a kiss on his nose, and he growled.

"I am claiming you in the true Hakron manner as my Male."

He went still. "I do not understand. I thought you were ashamed of our forced mating, ashamed of me."

"Gods, no! I thought you were mine from the moment I met you, but there's all this other stuff going on and you're..." She paused. "You're way out of my league."

"What does that mean?"

"It's an Earth saying. It means you are superior to me in every way."

"You jest. I am nothing."

She framed his face with her hands, aware of his heat and strength still throbbing inside her. "You are one of the bravest men I have ever met."

His gaze became distant. "I failed to escape the Etruscans. They used me for years. I have no worth as a warrior. I am *nothing.*"

"You survived. You *won.*"

"And in doing so, I put you in danger."

She grinned at him. "I'm a soldier. Danger is my middle name."

He didn't seem to understand that, so she focused on convincing him another way by slowly rocking her hips and riding him into a blaze of desire that would consume them both.

Suddenly he rolled and loomed over her. She was no lightweight, but she always forgot how big he was until he was on top of her.

"Be careful, Mya. If you claim me I will be yours forever."

She stroked his chest. "I'm good with that, but when we get to the Temple, we'll speak to the Oracle and to my other Male and make certain, okay?"

"Your other Male?"

"Yeah. Orin."

With a soft curse he pounded into her and they came together, minds aligned, bodies in perfect harmony she wished could go on forever.

"WHAT THE FRAK?" Orin muttered as he woke up suddenly in the uncomfortable interview room chair, his cock hard, his breathing ragged. They'd left him there to check out his credentials, which was krallshit, seeing as they could do that in a nanosecond. He reckoned he'd pissed off someone higher up by being at the right place at the right time when the local cops were taking a nap.

Thank the Gods there was no one there to witness his hard-on. Mya was close, and she was fucking another male with such intensity that he could almost taste it. What the heeze was going on? Had she gone nuts, or had she just decided she was done with him and found her own lover?

Whatever it was, he needed to get out of this jail and onto the streets before Mya disappeared again.

The door opened and an unknown man came in. He wore the uniform of the Pavlovan Special Forces and had the coldest blue eyes Orin had ever seen.

"Lieutenant Mazra? I do apologize for keeping you waiting here for so long. I was only just apprised of your intervention in the events that went down today and had to fly in from base."

Orin stood up. The man's accent was offworld, and he'd definitely met him before. "You work with my Female, correct?"

"Yes. I'm Lieutenant Roberts."

"The guy who was also on the mission to the Etruscan moon, right?"

"Would you care to sit down again? There are some things you really need to know."

6

———

MYA GROANED AS SHE WASHED HER HAIR. AS PREDICTED, ONE DAY after the attack on the restaurant she was sore as hell. An outstanding night of sex with Rekk hadn't helped, but she didn't regret that. He was hers. She was sure of that. Rinsing out the suds, she considered what to do next.

The security guys who had been assigned to them at the beginning of the trip had either been withdrawn or terminated. After the deliberate bombing of the restaurant, she suspected the latter, which left her with a dilemma. Should she and Rekk proceed as planned, or alter their course? If one of the security team had given away their route, they were screwed. She was beginning to see why Major Esca was determined to start a new elite security corps.

Instinct told her to change things up, and she wasn't going to argue with that. She'd kept her shields high, sharing only with Rekk, and was reluctant to seek any help. If someone wanted to contact her again, she would only settle for dealing with a real person, preferably a face she recognized.

She dried off and put the restaurant T-shirt back on over her black pants. Rekk was still sleeping, the long line of his naked body a lure that drew her to the side of the bed. She wanted to lick her way down his spine and…

"Be my guest."

He rolled onto his back and smiled up at her, one hand wrapped around his impressive morning erection.

"I have to go and do a few errands. I think it's better if we're not seen together for a while." She sat next to him and stroked his golden hair. "Will you be okay?"

"If you leave me a weapon with which to defend myself, I will contrive." He took her hand, the pale green of her skin stark against his more golden tones. "What do you need to do?"

"Get us some new clothes for one. We both look and smell like we've been in an explosion."

He chuckled, the sound so rich it made her nipples harden. His gaze dropped to her T-shirt and he cupped her breast. "Are you quite certain that you have to go right now?"

She removed his hand. "Yes. I'll be a quick as I can."

***

REKK CONTEMPLATED the locked door and whether it was worth getting up before Mya returned. He was strangely reluctant to wash her scent from his skin and hoped to lure her back into bed anyway. He fingered the weapon she had given him and ran through the list of instructions to make it work. Apparently, now she had tuned it to his *frequencies,* it would only fire for him and for her. He should perhaps have mentioned that he had never used such a weapon before… The idea that you could kill so many times and so quickly didn't sit well with him. Where was the honor in that?

A sound outside made him sit up. Before he had a chance to do much more, the door opened and a dark-haired man came through, his weapon pointed right as Rekk's head. He looked like he knew exactly how to kill a man.

"What have you done with my mate?"

Rekk put his weapon on the pillow. There was no point in pretending he would fire it now, and the male in front of him was far too intriguing to kill. "I will not harm you."

"As if you could. I'll give you ten seconds to give me some answers, and then I'll start shooting bits off—starting with your cock, seeing as I can smell my woman all over you."

Rekk put one hand over himself. "I am rather partial to my cock, and Mya seems to like it as well."

"Which makes no sense, seeing as she's mine."

"A Pavlovan citizen can mate with whomever he or she pleases until a permanent Triad is formed. Has that changed?" Rekk raised an eyebrow. "Has she erred?"

The male didn't even react as he shut the door behind him. "Your opinion isn't required. Where's Mya?"

"She will be back momentarily." Rekk gestured at the chair beside the desk. "Perhaps you should take a seat and await her return?"

"Perhaps I should shoot you in the head and walk away."

"And leave Mya to find me dead? That would not reflect well on either of us."

"Particularly you." The male sat down and glared at Rekk. He had hard eyes and a lean face with slanting cheekbones. "Why are you being so calm and reasonable?"

"You would prefer it if I panicked and attempted to shoot *you*?" Rekk shrugged. "I have to assume you are telling the truth, and that I have nothing to fear from you."

"Then you're wrong."

"If you had been sent by the Etruscans to end my existence, I would be dead by now. You came for Mya's sake." He paused, his eye on the weapon that was still leveled at his head. "You must be Orin."

"She *told* you about me?"

"She said she was mated to a male called Orin. That is all."

Rekk swung his legs over the side of the bed, and his guest tensed. "I am not going to do anything more threatening than take a shower. If that is permitted."

"You can stay right there until Mya gets back. If she doesn't get back, we'll be talking again. Otherwise shut the heeze up."

"As you wish."

Gods…

Orin tried not to gawk as the most beautiful man he had ever seen outside a porn vidscreen sank back onto the bed and clasped his hands in his lap. His skin was golden, as was his hair; his muscle definition was that of a pro athlete, and Orin reckoned he was way taller than average.

No wonder Mya had fucked him.

He shifted restlessly on the hard seat. And it wasn't just that the male was stunning, his mind was… Orin snapped his shields closed, but even then the man's telepathic power seeped through like warm syrup, making him want to lick him, lick that skin, walk over to that bed and just touch all that sleek, golden nakedness.

His captive sighed and relaxed, his posture that of a man used to waiting, which made Orin want to shoot him just because… Yeah, he was being totally professional about this demi-god who was fucking his mate.

The door latch clicked. Orin spun around, his weapon leveled at the door as Mya came in, her hands full of bags. She immediately dropped them on the floor.

"*Orin?*"

"Don't go for your weapon or I'll shoot him. Shut the door."

She kicked the door shut with her heel and turned to the man on the bed.

"Are you okay? Did he hurt you?"

"No. I could not find it within myself to use the weapon you left me. He accepted my surrender very graciously."

The guy spoke like someone out of a history book. Orin didn't get it at all, and Lieutenant Roberts's explanation about the situation hadn't provided useful information. All Roberts had said was that he would find Mya at this particular hotel and then he should await further instructions. He had only the most basic information about the golden god his mate was apparently fucking.

The male Orin's Female was currently rushing over to the bed to check on.

"Mya, what the heeze are you doing?" Orin snapped.

She had the nerve to turn around and glare at him. "Put your weapon away right now, Orin. This is ridiculous! You're supposed to be at the Temple."

"Rather than busting up your fuckfest?"

She went still and the male on the bed tensed. "It's not like that."

"It never is, is it? I'm a cop, Mya. I've heard every excuse in the universe."

She raised her chin. "I am not making excuses. You have blundered into a situation you do not understand. I am not allowed to share the details with you, so maybe you should just get out."

He returned her glare with one of his own. "How do you think I found you?"

"We are mated. I doubt it was hard."

"Well you'd be wrong about that because your boyfriend here has been shielding you both so carefully, I had no idea where you were until that explosion went off in the square."

"You were there?" She took a step toward him. "Did you see who did it?"

"I was more concerned about searching for you than

worrying about finding the perps. I'm supposed to be on vacation, remember?"

She sighed, her shoulders relaxing. "Orin, I'm sorry you are angry. I understand why, but if you had just stuck to our plan..."

"And met you at the Temple once you'd dumped lover boy and pretended to be all invested in finding our Third again?" He holstered his weapon. "Heeze, maybe I was a fool to hope you'd forgiven me and were ready to move on to the next part of our life together. I really screwed up, didn't I?"

The man on the bed rose to his feet and stood beside Mya, one hand on her shoulder. Gods, he was tall, towering over his mate. "Perhaps I could take my shower now and leave you both to settle your affairs? I promise I won't leave and I will respect your privacy as a mated couple."

Mya patted his hand. "Please don't. I still have a duty to keep you safe."

His smile was so intimate it made Orin's teeth hurt. He nodded. "Go ahead. I appreciate your tact."

The male's golden gaze fastened on Orin and he almost forgot how to breathe. "But do not hurt her. If you do, I will snap your neck with my bare hands."

With a nod, he went into the tiny bathroom and shut the door. Within seconds, the shower came on.

Mya sank down on the unmade bed and briefly closed her eyes.

"I know you won't believe me, Orin, but—"

"You're on a mission. I know. Lieutenant Roberts gave me your location."

"*Roberts*? Whatever for?"

"Because your primary security team got blown to pieces. I'm your back up."

She digested that, her head down, her gaze on the scuffed carpet. "Okay. What are we supposed to do next?"

"You're not going to shout at me?" Orin asked slowly.

"Why would I?"

"Because I'm interrupting...this." He gestured at the bed.

Her cheeks darkened as if he'd embarrassed her. "*This* was not supposed to happen. You know how I feel about getting close to anyone."

He tried to make a joke of it even as his heart stuttered. "So apart from the fact that he looks like a God and has more telepathic power in his little finger than I have in my entire person, what do you see in him?"

"I think he's our Third."

"But you've always hated the idea of having a Third."

"True."

"You're kidding. He's..." Orin blew out a breath. "He's way too powerful and there's something weird going on around him —it's like he's not from this time. And the way the Senate is intent on protecting him? He's not *normal,* Mya."

"I *know.* I can't explain it. But I also know he's ours."

"Maybe he's just yours, Mya."

She blinked at him. "You don't feel anything?"

"How could I not? He's like some kind of addictive drug. *Everyone* is going to be affected by him."

"That's what I thought at first, but—"

Orin moved to crouch in front of her. "Mya, I lied about not knowing much. Roberts told me what happened to you on the Etruscan moon. He said you'd been forced into a mating state." He took a breath. "This might all be because of that, *right?* You are aware of that?" He reached out to take her hand. "I'm not judging you or anything. I get it. But you have to admit this is so out of character for you—maybe there is some residual—"

She snatched her hand away. "No." She stood, rocking him back on his heels. "He's more to me—to *us* than that. I'm sorry, Orin, I know I'm not making much sense. Part of me wishes that I'm just imagining things. I don't understand it myself yet, but at some level I just *know* he's meant to be part of our future."

"Then try to understand where I'm coming from, okay?" He contemplated her for a long moment. "Everything I know about you tells me otherwise. We've been together for ten years, and I've never seen you so emotional or so fixated on something."

And at some level that hurt, but he refused to get into that now. He had to keep calm—had to get through to her.

"I'm fine, Orin." She took a quick breath. "I'm going to get Rekk to the Temple and I'm going to prove I'm right."

He rose slowly to his feet and faced her. "And if you're wrong?"

"Then you can call me a liar and ask for our union to be dissolved."

"*What?*" He realized he was shouting. "What the frak has gotten into you?"

She didn't back down. "That's how certain I am, Orin. I don't want to lose you—I love you, but I have to see this thing with Rekk through to the end. I'm probably wrong, but one thing almost losing my life on that Etruscan moon taught me was that at some point I'm going to at least have to try to be brave." She turned away. "Now I'm going to check on Rekk, and, if you're staying, we can get something to eat."

"I'm staying." He returned to his seat by the desk and sat down with a thump. "I promised that Roberts guy I'd see you safely to the Oracle."

She gave him a cool nod and knocked on the bathroom door, which immediately opened for her. If Rekk was their mate, and that was about as likely as Orin being voted into the Senate, the God-like one could have picked up their entire conversation telepathically. If he had been polite and respected their shields, he might have been listening at the door the whole time. Rekk didn't emerge. Orin didn't even want to think about what might be going down in there. His dick had other ideas, and he smoothed an impatient hand over the inconvenient bulge in his pants.

Nothing was what it seemed. His Female wasn't herself, he was stuck babysitting the most powerful telepath he had ever met, and his whole life had just turned upside down.

REKK STUDIED Orin's grim expression as they walked through the town to another public pick-up point for the transit system. Mya was walking ahead of them, her head covered to help her disguise. The male was about the same height as Mya and built on lean lines. Not that he looked puny—his muscularity was more akin to a lightning-fast predator than a weakling.

He was interesting…

"Are you in the military as well, Orin?"

"I'm a cop."

Rekk considered that. "What exactly do you do?"

"Day-to-day policing of my city."

"Ah. A peacekeeper, then."

This surprised a reluctant chuckle out of his companion. "You could say that."

"It is a worthy occupation."

Silence fell as they trudged through the mud that had gathered at the side of the road. It was still early in the morning and barely light. The thought of the three of them spending more than one night in one small space had made Mya decide to move out straight after breakfast. Rekk couldn't decide how he felt about that. He would've liked more time to spend getting to know Orin—not that the male seemed in any way likely to accept his friendship. He'd had his shields up permanently since they'd met.

Rekk sighed, and Orin glanced his way.

"It's not much further."

"Thank you for your concern. I am unused to walking."

"Yeah? You look in pretty good shape to me."

Mayhap the male had noticed him after all…

"I was trapped in one room for many years. They forced me to exercise, but it is not the same as being free to walk where you will."

Silence. Rekk tried again. "I am grateful to Mya for finding and rescuing me."

"So I hear."

"She is not to blame for any of this. Her first thoughts were for you. She was forced to mate with me. I have no claim on her."

"Yeah? That's not what she says."

Rekk stopped walking. "She believes I colluded in her capture?"

"*No*, you idiot, she—"

Mya turned around and came back to stand in between them.

"What's going on?"

"Nothing," Orin said. "Just shooting the breeze as the humans say."

She eyed them both suspiciously. "We need to get going. The first train leaves soon, and we have to buy new tickets."

"Then I shall walk faster." Rekk said. "The fault is mine."

Orin picked up his pace, stepping in front of Rekk and joining Mya. Rekk set his teeth and focused on the lights of the transit station ahead. He really was unused to walking. Once they were on the train, mayhap he could sleep and forget the complications surrounding him for just a little while.

ORIN GRUNTED as Mya elbowed him hard in the ribs. "What?"

"Why are you being so horrible to him?"

"To your fuck buddy?"

"Don't call him that." She scowled at him, the green of her skin darkening. "He is innocent."

"Funny, that's what he said about you. Weird how you end up fucking each other's brains out, and yet neither of you are to blame."

"You are acting like an asshole." She shoved him aside and focused on the ticket machine. "Can you make sure he's okay? I'll meet you on the platform."

Orin sighed elaborately. "Fine."

It was cold this early in the morning, and his breath condensed in the air as he looked around for Rekk. For a moment, he couldn't see him and he tensed before tentatively dropping his shields. Crap. There he was in all his lush, beckoning, sex-on-legs beauty…

Rekk raised a hand. Orin's cock twitched as he wordlessly made his way over to the bench where Rekk was sitting.

"Mya's getting the ticket credits." Orin sat down beside Rekk. "She's got to use good old-fashioned untraceable cash, so that's why it's taking a while."

Rekk just nodded, his golden gaze locked on the ground. What the frak was he supposed to say to the other male? It was like he wanted to touch him so badly, yet he knew it would be a mistake. Was that how Mya had felt? Like she just couldn't stop herself?

"Mya was forced into a mating state."

Dear Gods, this was bad. Rekk was inside his head despite his shields being at one hundred percent. And, even worse, he wanted him there, wanted to luxuriate in his power, roll around in it, strip him naked and....

"I am sorry."

"What for?" Orin didn't dare reply telepathically. He'd betray way too much.

"My captors operated on my shields. Sometimes I am unable to

stop my thoughts from flowing outward. I am trying to rebuild my skills."

"Okay."

He didn't want to be shut out. He wanted to be dragged in deeper despite himself.

"Orin?"

He took a deep breath and stood up. "Mya's coming and so is the train. Let's get onboard."

7

———

"Rekk, wake up."

He groaned as a sharp elbow connected with his ribs.

"*Rekk.*"

"What is it?"

He opened his eyes to find Orin tugging at his shirt..

"Mya thinks we picked up some company at the last stop."

"Etruscan company?" Dread flooded his gut.

"Yeah, so we're going to move out. Keep your head down and follow Mya. I'll be right behind you, okay?"

Rekk made sure the hood of his jacket covered his distinctive hair and zipped up the front, shoving his hands deep in the pockets as he slid out of his seat to stand behind Mya. He didn't dare use his telepathic abilities. He was fairly certain that his potential captors would home in on his signal in a second.

"Let's go get breakfast," Mya announced with a smile. "I'm starving!"

She started moving and so did he and Orin. Ahead of them, he could smell cooking food and beverages, which made his uneasy stomach rumble even more. They passed through two of the moving carriages and then paused outside the third, where he could see a line of passengers at a counter and some tables running down one side.

"How long until the next stop?" Orin asked quietly.

"Too long." Mya's fingers tapped against the doorframe. "We're going to have to get ourselves off this train."

"At this speed?" Orin frowned as he looked at the countryside flashing by the window.

"If we can connect into the automatic locomotion system we can probably slow it down enough for us to jump."

"You don't think the transit system has defenses against that?" Orin countered.

Mya's smile was grim. "Sure they do, but we have Rekk."

They both looked at him, and he shrugged. "I am willing to do whatever you require of me."

"You remember when we were in that bathroom, and we joined our hands so I could get into the security system?" Mya said.

"Yes." He remembered many things about that particular moment. He glanced at the other man. From the look on Orin's face, he was also getting way more information than he wanted.

Mya took his hand and placed it palm down on the control panel next to the exit door. She put her hand over his and turned to Orin.

"Come on."

"I doubt you need me."

"Orin..."

He placed his hand over Mya's. All three of them gasped as a bolt of heat pulsed through them.

"Okay, let's be quick. There's someone coming through the doors of the last carriage."

Rekk only had time for a quick glance back down the train to see that she was correct, and that one of the males was raising his hand and was probably armed.

"*Now.*"

Power pulsed around them, and the train slowed.

"Watch out!" Orin shouted as something whizzed past Rekk's shoulder and chaos erupted. He took up a firing position as Mya worked on the lock of the door.

"Got it. Let's go."

The next thing Rekk knew, Orin shoved him and he was falling and rolling down a steep bank. He had just enough time to draw himself into a tight ball and close his eyes as the train thundered into a tunnel, alarms blaring, and disappeared. His breath was forced out of him as he finally stopped moving and lay on his back, staring up at a particularly vivid blue sky.

A second later, Orin blundered into him. Rekk grabbed hold of his jacket to stop him going any further. He grunted as he took the man's weight and banged his head on the ground again. For a long while all he did was breathe in and out, which wasn't easy because Orin's face was tucked into his shoulder, and every labored breath he took meant he inhaled more of the male's scent.

Eventually, Orin groaned and attempted to lift his head, his blue gaze fuzzy.

"Frak. You okay down there, Rekk? Thanks for catching me."

Rekk cleared his throat. "I am… well."

"Where's Mya?"

"I have no idea."

Orin grimaced. "Yeah, seeing as I've got you pinned to the ground that was a pretty dumb question." He placed his hand on Rekk's chest and attempted to lever himself off before collapsing back. "Frak. I think I've damaged my ankle."

In one smooth motion, Rekk rolled them both over and gently lowered Orin to the ground, straddling his hips.

"Let me look." He ran his hands down over Orin's thighs and calves. "Where exactly does it hurt?"

"When you do that? Nowhere."

Rekk paused to look over his shoulder. "I do not understand."

"When you touch me? It's distracting."

"But my shields are up."

"It doesn't make any difference. I can still feel you."

"Then perhaps I should stop, and—"

"No. It's my problem." Orin grabbed his wrist. "Check my left ankle, okay?" His breath hissed out as Rekk curved a hand around the obviously swollen flesh. "My boot caught on something on the way down, and my foot got twisted around."

"Wait." Rekk concentrated. "I don't think it is broken, just sprained."

"Great," Orin muttered. "How about you go find Mya and bring her here so we can regroup and get moving again?"

"If you *can* move."

"I'll do whatever is necessary. Don't worry about me."

Rekk got unsteadily to his feet. Further down the slope, he spotted another figure and waved. Mya waved back, and to his relief, scrambled toward him.

"You guys okay?" she called.

"Orin has twisted his ankle."

She winced. "Frak. Can he walk?"

Rekk offered her his hand to help her up the last few steps of the bank. "Come and find out for yourself."

***

Mya left Orin's shoe in place and wrapped the bit of his ankle she could see with strips torn off her T-shirt. From the way he set his jaw, he was in considerable pain but determined not to say anything.

She consulted her internal map and checked their position. "There's a town just over this hill. We'll head there and find somewhere to stay."

Rekk nodded, his worried gaze fixed on Orin, who was attempting to stand. Without her saying anything, he took Orin's arm and wrapped it around his neck. She took up her position on Orin's other side.

"We can do this."

It seemed to take forever to get down the slope. The whole time, Mya was aware of the hairs on the back of her neck twitching as she anticipated another Etruscan attack. Why the hell did they want Rekk back so badly? She supposed only the Oracle would be able to help them answer that, and, if they didn't get under cover soon, they might never get far enough to find out.

"Building right on the edge of town is a hotel," Rekk said quietly. "Is it too obvious?"

"I don't think it matters at this point, do you?" Orin answered for her. "How many threesomes comprised of a green-skinned Hakron, a blond God, and a limping cop are going to be hanging out around here? Once we get a room, at least we can protect ourselves and call in reinforcements."

"He's right." Mya fixed her gaze on the brightly lit hotel sign. "Let's go for it."

It was an automated hotel with no visible staff. With Rekk and Orin shielding her thoughts, all she had to do was pick up the keycard from a box in the lobby using the password supplied in her reservation. Just to be on the safe side, she booked two rooms and took both keycards. They could choose the best defensible space.

At least Orin still had his weapons, although they'd left the backpack containing their clothes on the train. There was nothing in the pack that would help their pursuers.

They picked the room on the ground floor corner that faced the rear of the hotel. It was quiet round the back and there were several escape routes into the forest if they were attacked. It was also easier for Orin if he had to move fast.

"Let's go in." Mya went first, her weapon out. Rekk brought Orin in and gently sat him on the side of the bed as she checked out the bathroom.

"All clear."

Orin groaned and lay back on the pillows, his face white with pain. Mya locked the door and sat beside him. She took his hand.

"Do we need to get you a doctor?"

"Nope. I just need to get this damned shoe off and ice the joint."

"I'll go get some ice and see if there are any shops around." Mya immediately went back to the door. "Can you help Orin if he needs anything, Rekk?"

"Yes." Rekk nodded. "Unless you think I should accompany you."

"I'm good and I'll be less conspicuous on my own."

ORIN SLOWLY SAT up and stared down at his damaged foot, which Rekk had propped up on a pillow. Of all the times for him to get injured, this had to be the worst.

"Rekk, I have a knife in my pocket. Cut the laces."

He handed over the knife and waited as Rekk fixed his attention on the damage.

"It will be better if I can untangle the knots. You will need the shoe again at some point."

"Sure, whatever, just get it done."

"I'll be as careful as I can."

"Yeah, don't cut anything that looks like a toe or anything useful, okay?"

Rekk smiled. "Your sense of humor is remarkable."

Orin attempted a shrug. "I'm a police officer. We live and die by our stupid jokes."

"I should imagine that is true." Rekk carefully worked on another loop of the tangled lace. "Calling me a blond god was another of your jokes, yes?"

"No."

Rekk went still. "Then it was an insult?"

"You're kidding, right? You ever look in the mirror, big boy?"

"I try not to. All I see is a stupid fool who allowed himself to be held captive for years and… used."

"From what I hear escaping wasn't an option."

"I tried in the early days, but every time they caught me they made things worse." He grimaced. "I spent so many days trapped in a small, dark space with no contact with another being that I thought I would go mad. Eventually I gave up and let them do what they wanted." His smile was brief. "There is probably not a creature on Pavlovan who is less godlike than I am."

On impulse, Orin reached out and cupped Rekk's chin. "I don't see a coward. I see a survivor."

With a stifled sound, Rekk brushed his lips across Orin's thumb. "Poor Mya, having to drag me across country when she wishes to be with you—an honorable male."

"I don't think she sees it like that." Orin tried to ignore the way the blood was sizzling in his veins and his cock was thickening. He really should let go of Rekk's chin. "I fucked up before she left on her last mission. I'm surprised she's even speaking to me."

"You did?"

"Yeah. I tried to push her into finding our Third."

To his relief, it was Rekk who sat back. "She did not wish to complete your Triad?"

He shrugged. "She has some… issues about Triads. She's never told me exactly what went down in her family, but I guess it was bad."

He should have asked her. He should have gotten the truth

out of her years ago instead of pretending it would never be a problem.

Rekk returned to working on releasing his foot, and silence fell between them.

"I wish I could go back ten years and start again," Orin blurted out.

"To when you were first mated to Mya?"

"Yeah. We were both so young when we met."

"Mayhap we all have regrets? They do say hindsight is a wonderful thing. I suspect I wouldn't have been so eager to get away from my family obligations and explore the universe if I'd known where I'd end up." Rekk's smile was wry.

Orin's breath hissed as Rekk eased his mangled foot out of the remains of his shoe.

"Damn. That looks bad," Orin muttered.

Rekk hesitated, his hand hovering over the swollen ankle. "I could try something."

"Like what?"

"My family has some healing abilities. If you will permit me to lay my hands on you?"

Orin wanted to tell him to lay his entire body on him, but he'd take anything he could get. "Sure. Knock yourself out."

"I don't think it will come to that, but my powers are rather depleted at the moment." Rekk closed his eyes and took a long, slow breath. Inside Orin's head, a soft, glowing force saturated his thoughts. "Yes. I can feel…"

As the heat of Rekk's power flowed through Orin's bones, he grabbed hold of the other man's shoulder and held on for dear life.

"Almost done," Rekk murmured.

Orin tightened his grip. "Why don't you ever talk to me telepathically?"

Rekk's startled gaze flew to his face. "Because you asked me not to."

"When?"

"When we first met you suggested my power was over-whelming you. It's all right. My shields are not working properly, and those who get close to me are bombarded with too much… me."

Orin moved his hand into Rekk's hair. "And what if I wanted to be bombarded?"

"I do not understand."

Orin cursed under his breath and brought his mouth to Rekk's. The kiss turned crazy hot within a second as Rekk parted his lips and let Orin's tongue tangle with his own. With a strangled sound, Orin shoved Rekk down onto the bed and climbed on top of him, hard cock rubbing against hard cock, minds finally, *finally*, totally in sync.

The sound of footsteps outside the door made Rekk shove him away hard. Orin ended up on the floor without really knowing how he got there. By the time Mya came through the door, Rekk had disappeared into the bathroom and Orin was climbing painfully back onto the bed.

"You okay?" Mya flew to his side. "Did you fall?"

"Yeah, kind of."

She helped him sit up and looked down at the ruins of his shoe and then his foot.

"Wow. It looks a lot better than I thought it would."

Orin waved a vague hand toward the bathroom. "Rekk did some healing stuff on it."

"Rekk did? Is he all right?"

"How the heeze should I know? Ask him when he comes out." Mya continued to study him. "*What?*"

"You're really agitated. Do you have a fever or something?"

Only in my balls. Orin forced himself to lie back against the pillows. "I'm just tired. Did you get any supplies?"

Thank the Gods that managed to distract her long enough

for him to get under the covers and give his dick a stern talking to.

"Do you think they'll follow us here?" he asked.

"Probably." Mya was busy pulling stuff out from her bag. "Is there any way we can call for back up?"

"Not from my lot. The lines are too public."

"My so-called security team disappeared in Paloma. I'll see if Rekk can help me contact Roberts."

"The guy from Earth with the odd telepathic abilities?"

"The humans I've met here are all like that." She grimaced. "Some kind of military program messed with their brains and natural telepathic abilities. Sometimes it's like communicating with a robot rather than a man."

"That sucks."

"I think Rekk would agree with you." She looked over at the bathroom. "He's been in there quite a while. Do you think I should go and check on him?"

"Up to you." Orin shrugged. If he went in there and Rekk was naked in the shower, he wouldn't be any help hurrying him along at all... Gods, when had his thoughts degenerated into imagining soaping and sucking another male's dick? He'd always thought their Third would be a woman.

"Orin..."

He looked at Mya who was now right by the bathroom.

"I don't hear anything."

"Knock."

She did and then called Rekk's name before cautiously turning the handle. "It's locked."

"And I don't sense him anymore, do you?" Orin leapt off the bed hoping his ankle was good enough to bear his weight. He joined Mya at the door, pressing his ear against the wood.

"Talk to him."

"Why, what do you think he's done?"

"Gone." He crouched down and inserted the corner of his

plastic special-issue police keycard into the tiny gap between the door and the frame. He pulsed a thought through it and heard the lock snap open.

"But why?"

Orin groaned as he painfully straightened up. "Probably because I kissed him."

"What?" Mya grabbed his arm. "*Why?*"

The bathroom was empty and Orin's gut turned over. "Let's worry about that later."

8

He was a fool and a liability. Rekk finally stopped running when he was deep within the trees, bending down to gasp in some much needed air. He was definitely the loudest thing in the forest. He hoped there weren't any large prey animals in this part of the world because, if there were, he was probably being tracked and would soon be dead.

"At least I'd serve a useful purpose," he muttered as he straightened up. His gaze swept the mottled greens and browns of the woodland and moved upward until he was staring at a small patch of blue sky. "At least I'll die a free man."

If he were no longer with Mya and Orin, they would be safe. That he was sure about. Being with him was dangerous, not only because he was being so relentlessly pursued, but because he couldn't hide his telepathic abilities. Poor Orin had been as mesmerized as Mya. His kiss… Rekk licked his lips. Orin's hard cock… his *mind.*

That was what he turned people into, and he *hated* it. That's why he'd been captured and kept. Because he couldn't keep his thoughts in check.

Something flew overhead, shattering the silence, and he

instinctively ducked. He had no plan. All he wanted was to be left alone. Maybe, when Mya and Orin left, he could carry on his journey to the Temple alone. His returning memory meant he had some sense of where he was now and in what direction he needed to travel. He would have to cross Hakron and Nevek territory, but those groups tended to keep to themselves. He would do his best to avoid contact with anyone.

Finding a large tree, he hunkered down at the base, stretched out his legs and leaned back, trying to relax. Mya and Orin were trained military professionals. He had no doubt that whatever they faced, they would win. But what if the Etruscans left them alone and simply came after him? He'd rather that happened than his protectors get hurt.

He wouldn't be taken back alive. That was a given. If necessary, and if he couldn't avoid the Etruscans, he would provoke them into killing him.

He'd loved being outside when he was a boy and hated being dragged into the house for his lessons by his tutor. As he'd grown older, his duties and his lessons had increased to such an extent that he'd rarely seen daylight. Rekk frowned. Duties for what? He couldn't remember anything directly before the space flight and the crash when the Etruscans had captured him. He'd escaped one prison for one that was far worse.

Had they wiped his mind deliberately? He could see why that might have appealed not only to their scientists, but also to the woman who used him as her sexual toy. Maybe they'd taken his memories repeatedly, which was why he no longer recognized anything around him and only had flashes of his past.

"Don't move."

He flinched as the barrel of a weapon jammed hard against the side of his neck.

The accent was Etruscan. The voice unfamiliar.

The man searched him for weapons. Something about the

rough way he shoved his hand under Rekk's T-shirt was enough to set off his simmering rage.

"No more!"

With a savage growl, he head-butted the man in the stomach, smacking the weapon away.

With a startled yelp, the soldier staggered backward, falling on his ass, and Rekk was all over him, wrenching the weapon from his hand and holding it against his temple.

"Rekk? I'm right behind you. Don't shoot."

He stared down at the soldier's terrified face. Had he ever killed anyone before? He couldn't even remember that.

Orin touched his shoulder, his voice gentle. "I've got this, buddy. Let me deal with him."

Rekk nodded once and let Orin take control of the weapon and the prisoner. Orin knocked the man out and tied him up, his movements efficient and practiced.

"I know you want to kill him, and I totally understand why, but if he dies the rest of the Etruscan pack will know instantly, and they'll be all over us." Orin tightened the man's gag. "This way he can stay put for a while longer while we get away."

Rekk slowly rose to his feet. "I'm not coming with you."

"You want to stay here and wait for the Etruscans to take you back?"

He glanced down at the man's weapon. "I thought to provoke him into killing me or turning the weapon on myself."

"What the heeze for?" Orin snapped. "I just saved your ass!"

"Why?" Rekk demanded, stepping right into Orin's personal space. "You and Mya were supposed to leave. What are you doing here and where is Mya?"

"Mya is perfectly capable of taking care of herself."

"Whereas I am not?"

"We are your designated bodyguards. Our mission is to get you to the Temple."

"I don't want your damned help!"

"I'm not offering you any. I'm *telling* you I have to complete my mission!"

Rekk turned around and stormed off into the forest. Orin followed him.

"Where the frak are you going *now?*"

"Anywhere that you are not!"

Orin grabbed hold of his shirt, spinning him around. "You are staying with me."

"Why? So I can distort your thinking? Make you want to kiss me again?"

"Distort my *thinking?* Man, you do that, but—"

"It is *wrong*. I am not… worthy of your attention."

"Are you telling me I don't have the right to have feelings for you?"

Rekk growled. "You don't have feelings! *I* am the problem. I make you feel things that don't exist!"

"Yeah?" Orin twisted his fist into Rekk's T-shirt and yanked him so close there was no air between them. "You make me so fucking hard I can't think of anything but stripping you naked, offering you my ass or taking yours." He shook Rekk. "You think I want to feel like this about a man I'm supposed to be protecting with my life?"

All the anger drained from Rekk. "No. And that is the point I am trying to make. You don't *have* to feel like this. One day away from me and you will be back to normal. I corrupt everything I touch."

"You don't seriously believe that, do you? You think what I feel is nothing but something *you've* created?"

Rekk met Orin's outraged blue gaze. "You know it's the truth —my shields are damaged. I… attract people."

"So everyone you meet immediately wants to fuck you?"
He nodded.

"Wow, conceited much?" Orin shoved him in the chest. "Then listen up. I want to fuck you because you're mine."

"Orin…"

"Shut up." He stuck his finger right in Rekk's face. "You're mine and Mya's. When you work that out, you come and find me, and you'd better be on your knees begging to suck my dick." Orin checked his weapon. "Now come on, we're supposed to be meeting Mya in the next town. We can reach it through the woods."

Rekk tried again. "I think you and Mya would be safer without me."

"And *I* think you're talking out of your ass. Mya and I are under orders, and neither one of us likes to fail, so get a move on, soldier!"

Rekk started walking in the direction Orin pointed. He could work with this. Mya and Orin would get him to the Temple whether he liked it or not. Once they were there and separated, Orin would quickly recover from his infatuation and everything would be well. He wouldn't even think about his bond with Mya.

So if that was the case, why did he feel as if he were making a terrible mistake?

"*Incoming. Don't shoot—unless you want to shoot Rekk who's an ass for running off in the first place.*"

Thank the Gods. That was Orin's voice. Mya lowered her weapon but didn't put it away as she scooted off the bed and went to the side of the door. She unlocked the security code and stood back as Rekk was shoved into the room followed by Orin.

She immediately grabbed hold of Rekk's shoulders. "Are you okay? Why did you leave us?"

He swallowed hard. His face was muddy and his expression grim.

"I thought you would be better off without me bringing the Etruscans onto you."

"So noble and yet *so* fucking wrong," Orin muttered. "I told him it's our job to get him to the Temple. If he wants to be all heroic and shit after that, he can do what the frak he pleases."

Mya glanced over at Orin who was looking equally surly. "What's wrong?"

"Why would you think anything is wrong? I just love sneaking around the forest saving dickheads from shooting Etruscans in the head."

Rekk shoved a hand through his disordered blond hair. "I believe he is talking about me, although I am not certain what a dickhead is." Rekk looked from Orin to Mya. "I am sorry. I will not attempt to escape again. I will accept your escort to the Temple."

"Thanks for nothing." Orin turned on his heel. "I'm taking a shower."

Mya winced as the door slammed hard behind him. "Why is he in such an awful mood?"

Rekk sat on the edge of the bed and rubbed his hands over his face. "Because I told him to leave me in the forest, and he became angry for my lack of gratitude for his protection."

"That doesn't sound like Orin." Mya studied Rekk intently. "He's usually the calmest and most efficient man I've ever met in a crisis situation."

"I… annoy him."

"You certainly unsettle him, but that's not necessarily a bad thing. He does have a tendency to think he knows everything." Mya sat beside him and took his hand. "This is difficult for you, but we really do want to get you safely to the Temple."

"Yes, Orin said it was your mission, and that he doesn't like to fail."

"Now, that *is* just like him. You don't dislike him, do you?"

"Orin? No, on the contrary, I find much to admire in him. I only wish—"

The bathroom door opened and Orin came out, a small towel draped around his hips. Rekk stopped speaking and simply stared at the other man.

"What do you wish, Rekk?" Mya asked quietly.

He rose as if in a daze, his eyes fixed on Orin. "I should shower myself."

"You do that, Rekk. And this time don't leave out of the window." Orin didn't move aside, so Rekk had to push past him. "Don't take too long, or I'll have to come in there and find you."

Rekk nodded and went into the bathroom while Orin started to dry himself off.

"What's going on?" Mya said. "You're acting as if you hate him, and he's staring at you as if you are his favorite dessert."

Orin stopped long enough to fix her with a piercing blue stare. "Nothing happened, okay? And that's the way he wants it."

"Did you try to… kiss him again?"

"No."

"Did you want to?"

Silence greeted her question.

"Orin."

He crouched down by the bags containing the items she'd bought.

"Do you have any new underwear or a clean T-shirt in here?"

She came off the bed and hunkered down beside him, using her fingertips to catch the water rolling down his muscled back. He shivered.

"Don't do that."

"Why not?" She leaned in and licked the next drop. "This better?"

He groaned her name, and the next thing she knew, he was

on top of her and kneeing her thighs apart. His towel fell away to reveal the thick column of his shaft.

"I want you." He leaned in and kissed her, the wet crown of his cock nudging her stomach. "I've missed you so damn much, and I'm so damned sorry for—" His words ended in a grunt as she raised her hips, pushed down her clothing, and let him inside her. He fucked her fast and hard, just how she wanted it, needed it.

She wrapped her arms around his shoulders and held on tight, glorying in the feel of him, so different from Rekk, yet still hers.

"How's he different? He's bigger, right? Does he fuck you harder?"

"He's just different." Some devil made her add. *"You wait until he fucks you, you'll find out."*

He went still for a long moment and then increased his pace, slamming into her, his hips rocking back and forth.

"I... want that."

"It's okay, I want to see it, too."

"Gods... Don't admit it, I—"

He wrapped an arm around her hips, raising her even higher, and hammered into her. She spread herself wider, urging him on as he fingered her clit, sending her into a climax that made her want to scream with the pleasure of it. A movement over his shoulder caught her eye. Rekk stood in the open bathroom door, his cock hard and ready beneath his towel.

She held out a hand. "Join us."

"I cannot."

Orin spoke as well. "No, he can't join us. He knows the rules."

"What?" Mya stopped speaking as Orin resumed his relentless thrusts and this time he came with her, pushing his thoughts and his come inside her with everything he had.

REKK GROANED low in his throat, one hand wrapped around his straining cock. He had never seen anything as beautiful as the sight of Mya and Orin mating. He wanted to be with them, licking and sucking, fucking Orin's flexing ass...

"*Shut up.*" Orin growled inside his head. "*You don't get to do that until you beg.*"

Gods, it would be so easy to get down on his knees, crawl over to them, and *be* with them. But he'd sworn he'd never be reduced to begging again in his life.

"*I cannot.*"

Orin picked up Mya and carried her over to the bed. She was smiling and sated, the scent of Orin's lovemaking marking her skin.

"*Then sleep over there by yourself.*"

Rekk backed up until his knees hit the side of the second bed, and he abruptly sat down. He could still see them, but he didn't want to stop looking. He tried to remember that their infatuation with him was just that—not a lasting thing. What would happen when his telepathic skills were properly contained and he was no longer unduly influencing them? They'd be stuck with him, and he'd rather die than let that happen.

Mya kissed Orin and sat up. "I think I'm the one who needs to shower now." She moved slowly toward the bathroom, pausing to rest a hand on Rekk's shoulder. "Are you okay?"

"I am fine."

He waited until the door shut behind her, and then rolled onto his side facing the wall, his hand gripping his aching cock.

"*Do it.*"

He went still as Orin spoke in his head.

"*Share that with me, at least.*"

Closing his eyes, Rekk turned onto his back and unwrapped his towel. His cock jerked between his fingers as he played with himself, drawing his hips into each upward stroke, bending his knees so Orin could see him more clearly. Gods, he was so wet now he had to tighten his grip. His breath hissed out as the rhythm caught hold of him. He just gave himself to it, sharing every slick thrust and slide with Orin.

"*Gods...*" Orin murmured. "*You are so beautiful. Fuck yourself for me.*"

Rekk slid his wet thumb backward and worked it inside his ass, gasping as the sensations doubled, and he bucked in earnest.

"*Yeah, just like that. Now come for me.*"

At Orin's command he gave one last twist to his cock, cupped his balls and came hard, his come spilling out onto his stomach as he gasped for breath.

Orin sighed. "*I want to come over there and lick you clean.*"

"That would not be a good idea," Rekk said hoarsely.

"Not under our present agreement, no." Orin groaned. "Remind me why we're not all in a big pile fucking each other's brains out again?"

"Because we need to get to the Temple first."

"So you can convince yourself that anything Mya and I might feel is all imaginary and inspired by you."

"Yes."

"Just checking." Orin stretched out an arm and switched off his bedside light. "I'm going to sleep. Wake me in four hours."

9

MYA GLANCED BEHIND HER ON THE NARROW TRAIL TO CHECK that both Rekk and Orin were still following her. It was humid in the dappled sunlight, and even the huge trees didn't offer enough protection from the searing heat. She wiped the sweat from her face with her sleeve and took a long drink of water. As she'd grown up around the Temple complex, she knew several routes that were literally off the beaten track. She was fairly confident the Etruscans wouldn't be able to find them here. They must have brought one of their telepaths with them to succeed in tracing them this far.

Neither of the males looked particularly happy. In the three days since they'd left their last proper hotel room, they'd barely spoken to each other. From what Orin said, Rekk was determined not to believe in any kind of mating bond between them until he reached the Temple and found out who he was. But what if the Oracle didn't *know* who he was? Would he be more willing to trust her and Orin then?

Orin reached her first and stopped alongside her.

"How much further is it?"

"One more night and we'll be there early the next morning."

"Good." Orin drank some water, his gaze on Rekk who was coming up the steep path. "You okay?"

She gave him a look. "With you two behaving like school children? Not particularly."

He shrugged. "Not my fault. Ask Rekk."

"Ask me what?" Rekk loomed over her, his grey T-shirt clinging to his tight abs and chest like a second skin.

"When you're going to beg."

Rekk went still. "I am *never* going to beg."

"Why not? You think you're too good for us or something?"

Mya sighed. "Orin... don't do this now, okay?"

Rekk squared off against Orin. "I spent years chained in a room, begging to be freed, and then begging for someone, for anyone, to touch me! And if I did not beg for it, they gave me drugs to drive me mindless with lust so I had to, and..." He stopped speaking, his chest heaving. "They made me their whore. Is that what you want, Orin? Is that what you want of me? Because Gods help me, I'll probably do it. That's who I am. A begging, beautiful, worthless whore."

Mya pushed between the two men.

"Rekk, don't—that's not what he meant, and—"

Orin spoke over her. "He damn well knows that's not how I think of him!" Reaching forward, he jabbed Rekk in the chest. "I want you to *choose* to beg, to *choose* Mya and me, and you don't have the balls to do it, do you?"

"Stop it!" Mya shoved them both hard. "This is not the place for this!"

"Maybe it is," Orin countered. "Maybe we need to sort this out before we get there so the minute his ass in on Temple grounds we can walk away."

Mya briefly closed her eyes, one hand planted on each of their chests, straining to keep them apart. "I don't want to walk away from either of you, but I'll do it if you don't stop this right now! I cannot deal with it. I can't—"

With a sob she pushed past them both and started up the trail, her heart pounding and her legs like jelly.

"Mya!"

Orin's shout only made her move faster. She wanted to run away and hide like a little child, cowering in the corner. Blinking back tears, she evened out her breathing and settled into a smooth jog. There was no other path. The men would eventually catch up to her—if she let them—but she needed this small space to compose herself.

ORIN STARTED off after Mya but was yanked backward.

"Let her be."

"She's upset." Orin tried to get free. "We need to go after her."

"Let her *be.*"

He scowled at Rekk. "I've been her mate for ten years. Don't you think I know how to handle her?"

"Obviously not if your idea of making her happy is to start a fight with me in the middle of a jungle."

"You didn't exactly hold back, did you?"

Rekk grimaced. "I lost my temper—a luxury long denied me and maybe for a good reason." He looked up the trail and frowned. "Her thoughts are very hard to understand."

"She's probably blocking us both." Orin groaned. "I'm an idiot."

"No, it's not that—although her reflections on both of us are hardly flattering—she's frightened..."

"Of us?"

"No, of what we represent."

Orin finally stopped struggling to go after her. "What the heeze does that mean?"

"I'm not sure. Was her father an aggressive man?"

Orin blinked at Rekk. "I don't know. He was already dead

when I met Mya. Her mother had formed a new Triad." He paused. "You think we triggered something from her past?"

"What?" Rekk widened his eyes. "Two large males shouting at each other?"

"There's no need to be sarcastic. When did that happen?" Orin picked up his backpack. "Let's keep moving forward."

Within a few steps he started speaking again. "She's always been afraid of having a Third."

"Why?"

"I don't know. We'd always put off discussing it until just before all this shit went down. I was injured during a shoot-out, and my partner was killed. It made me think, you know?" He glanced over to see if Rekk was listening. "I told Mya I wanted to find our Third and maybe start a family."

"She did not react well to your suggestions?"

"She wasn't very happy. She's never wanted a baby. But she did agree to talk about it when she got back." Orin cleared his throat. "And then she met you, and now I don't know what to think."

"She is probably quite conflicted as well," Rekk suggested.

"Yeah, look at us. All three of us are screwed up about this situation in some way." Orin snorted. "Typical."

"Then perhaps we should find Mya, and maybe it is time to talk things through."

"*If* we find her," Orin muttered. "Remember, she grew up here. If we've really pissed her off, she could lead us around in circles for days."

He kept walking, mainly because there was nothing else he could do. Eventually, they reached a plateau of some kind. Rekk pointed out into the gathering darkness.

"Look. There is the Temple."

Orin stared across the deep valley at the pale, white stone of the Oracle's Temple complex. The lamps had already been lit, and thousands of them framed the beautiful buildings. He hadn't been here for ten years since his mating ceremony.

"This, at least, hasn't changed a bit," Rekk said slowly.

"Yeah, I think it's been the same for thousands of years. Thank the Gods."

Just the sight of the Temple gave Orin hope. The Oracle within was renowned for her ability to make Triad matches, discern the future, and perform the spiritual ceremonies that ensured the Pavlovian world still functioned. No one, not even the Senate or the Etruscans, had ever succeeded in destroying the Oracle or her Temple.

"There's a lot more security now." Orin pointed at the lower gates. "Since that last attack on the Oracle, the heir's mate Ian Mac has been implementing a whole series of new checks and levels to keep the Oracle safe."

"That is good to know."

"You'll be safe there."

"Thank you." Rekk offered him a half-smile.

"Now, let's find Mya."

THEY FOUND her sitting cross-legged in front of a fire, her bedding already laid out under a tree. She was stirring something in a pot that hung over the blaze. Rekk put his backpack down and went to stand opposite her.

"May I sit with you?"

She looked up and nodded. She had been crying. The sight of her reddened eyes made his gut clench.

"I wish to apologize for my outburst. It was uncalled for."

"But not unprovoked."

Orin hunkered down next to him. "I'm sorry, too, Mya. I'm an idiot."

Rekk was ashamed to say that Mya's lack of reaction to Orin's apology made him feel slightly more hopeful.

She ladled out whatever was in the pot onto three large leaves and offered them both one. Rekk curled the sides of the leaf up within his palm and slid the fragrant meat and fruit into his mouth.

"This is good. Thank you."

Orin paused with his hand close to his mouth. "Er, what exactly am I eating?"

"Best not to know out here." Rekk took another mouthful. "I'm too hungry to care."

Orin laughed. "Yeah." He nibbled at a chunk of meat. "Hey, it's good."

"Thank you." Mya had removed her jacket and released her hair around her shoulders. Her green skin blended in perfectly with the forest, making her look like some kind of tree spirit. If she had chosen to abandon them on the path, he doubted they would've been able to track her without their telepathic connection.

She set down her leaf and drank some water. "I am sorry as well."

"There is no need for you to apologize. We both behaved badly."

"But I overreacted." She shivered, wrapping her arms around herself. "I...don't respond well to aggression in males."

"Was that because of your father?" Orin asked.

Rekk just looked at him. *Really? You're just going to blurt it out like that?*

Why not?

Mya raised an eyebrow. "Why would you think that?"

Orin shrugged. "Just a theory."

"My father was an honorable man,"

Rekk studied her now-tense body language. "What about the

new member of your mother's Triad? Was he or she a good person?"

She slowly let out her breath. "No. He was not."

"Yet your mother stayed with him."

"She was Hakron. A vow once taken for a Hakron is a sacred thing." She drew her knees up to her chest and wrapped her arms around them. "She refused to leave until it was too late."

"What do you mean?" Orin asked.

"He killed her when he found out she was carrying his Second's child."

Rekk briefly closed his eyes to say a prayer for Mya's mother.

"The Second Male took me back to my father's village. I was raised there by my grandparents."

Orin leapt to his feet. "Why didn't I know this?"

"Because I was ashamed and the Hakron will not speak of these things." Despite her words, Mya met his gaze straight on, her bearing as regal as a queen's. "I didn't want you to know my mother had been murdered by her own mate."

"But I should have asked. I should have *known...*" Orin slapped the side of his head. "I am a complete loser as a Male and a mate!"

"You are not at fault." She swallowed hard. "I was going to tell you when I came back from my mission. I knew you wanted a Third and a baby and... I knew I had some issues with those things."

Orin came down on one knee in front of her. "Mya, if I'd known about this... I would never have pressed you at all."

She smiled shakily. "But it doesn't matter anymore, does it? Because whatever else happens between the three of us, I obviously have the ability to put my fear behind me and contemplate a new future with you two. Being close to death taught me something."

Rekk stared at her. How could she be so strong? He doubted

his own name, and she had the courage he lacked to move onward. But surely it made his decision to wait until he'd seen the Oracle more important? He could not betray Mya or Orin and let them down again.

He gathered his own courage. "If I am your choice, and if the Oracle can tell me *who* I am, then I will gladly ask you both if I am still acceptable as a Third."

"On your knees?" Orin asked.

Rekk gave him a wry look. "If I must."

MYA STUDIED the two men carefully. Neither of them seemed disturbed by the evidence of her violent past—their concern was all for her.

"I *am* afraid of being in a committed Triad and of having offspring." She offered the truth willingly now. "I always wondered if I might be too like my mother—too soft, too used to submitting to the old ways—which is why I suppose I went into the military to prove her and myself wrong."

"You are one of the strongest females I have ever met, Mya," Rekk said.

"I'd have to agree." Orin grinned at her. "You've never taken any shit from me and, apparently, I'm not easy to live with."

Impulsively, Mya reached out her hand to him. "You're my mate. I've always known you were on my side—even when I was afraid I couldn't live up to your expectations."

He frowned. "I would *never* have forced a child or a mate on you. You know what I'm like, Mya. I just hated not knowing what the problem was and how to solve it. I just rushed ahead, trying to do it all anyway."

"I know. I was more worried that I would give in—does that make sense? That I would somehow become my mother."

"How did the Oracle allow such a remarriage?" Rekk asked slowly.

"She does get it wrong sometimes." Mya took his hand as well. Somehow it seemed right. "But my mother didn't consult with her. She just made her decision and went with it."

He brought her hand to his mouth and kissed her palm. "May your mother have found peace in her rebirth with the Gods."

"Thank you."

Orin finished his food. "What happened to him?"

"To whom?"

"The man who killed your mother?"

"He's dead."

"Good, because otherwise I'd be finding him and having a few words about beating up on a defenseless pregnant women." Orin was all business now, the amusement gone from his face. "There is a special place in the underworld for vermin like that."

"Agreed." Rekk gathered the used leaves. "We should try to sleep. It will be a long day tomorrow."

Mya scraped out the pot and repacked her backpack. When she returned from washing out the utensils in the stream, Orin had banked up the fire and laid the other two sleeping mats on either side of hers. Her steps slowed as she considered the implications of the sleeping arrangements.

Rekk caught her eye. "I can sleep over there if you prefer it."

"No, I'd... like us all to be together on this final night. Things might never be the same after we meet the Oracle."

Rekk would find out that he was an aristocrat descended from the highest in the land, and that he'd been missing for over a hundred years. How would he feel then? Was it fair not to warn him that his humble offer to be their Third might seem laughable when he realized how far above them he was? She'd promised her superior officers not to reveal that information to him, but that was before he'd become so special to her and Orin.

Rekk moved away to take off his boots.

Orin spoke from behind her, his voice low. "We're going to lose him tomorrow, aren't we?"

"Possibly," Mya agreed. "But we can't stop him from reclaiming his birthright."

"Maybe he was right about us not making any promises before we saw the Oracle after all, but Gods, I just wish we'd all…"

Mya placed her finger on his lips and then replaced it with her mouth. His eyes widened, as she pressed close, her mind blending effortlessly with his.

"We have tonight… If he is willing."

He kissed her back. *"Let's go and see, shall we?"*

Rekk looked up as they approached, his gaze fixing on Mya's lips as if he was intent on tasting the shared kiss.

Mya pointed at the sleeping mat in the center. "This one is yours, Rekk."

"Are you sure?"

"Yeah." Orin knelt on the left mat at Rekk's level. "Lie down."

Rekk stretched out, his breathing uneven as if the force of their combined attention was difficult to take. Mya cupped his chin, turning his face toward her. He was truly beautiful, his wary gaze golden, his lips slightly parted as he regarded them both. But he was so much more than that. He had such strength and patience, things both she and Orin lacked. He would be their anchor and the very center of their bonded Triad. If he wanted them.

"As this is the end of our journey, the end of our mission, and perhaps the end of the world as we know it, perhaps we can finish in style?"

Rekk licked his lips. "In what way?"

"In a way that means we can all start fresh tomorrow?" She leaned in and kissed his nose, then each slanted cheekbone, and finally his luscious mouth. "With no regrets and without worrying about the future."

"Time out of mind," Orin suggested as he trailed his fingers down over Rekk's T-shirt, making him shiver. "One night to enjoy each other, no questions asked."

"Don't you think it will simply make things worse?"

"I don't think they could be much worse, do you?" Mya countered. "Orin and I both want to be with you so much. Are you willing?"

Rekk's eyes widened as Orin's roving finger settled on the already prominent bulge of his cock and made small circles.

"Just two Males and their Female enjoying a night of love-making together." Mya kissed him deep.

Orin snorted. "Yeah, that's us all right." He cupped Rekk's balls, his thumb rubbing up and down his shaft. "All I want at this moment is to have your cock in my mouth while I suck you off."

"Only if Rekk agrees, Orin," Mya spoke over her frank and unfiltered lover. "Only if his conscience allows it."

"What is it you fear for me tomorrow that you both offer me this gift?" Rekk said softly. "That I will go back on my word?"

"Consider this more as a hope that you won't. We want you to be happy, Rekk."

"You know I want you both."

"That's a start," Orin murmured. "Come on, Rekk. Let us love you just for one night. We really want to."

Rekk slowly exhaled. "Then I am yours."

Mya kissed him, easing her hand inside his T-shirt to pull it off him, exposing his long, golden limbs and muscular chest. Orin started work on his pants, coaxing the buttons to open to reveal the thick length of Rekk's already hard cock.

"Yeah," Orin breathed the word like a prayer and bent his head to lick and suck Rekk's skin as it slowly emerged from his pants. "Fucking nice."

Rekk groaned and arched his back, allowing Orin to pull down his pants completely. He kicked them off and lay naked before them. Mya couldn't contain a whimper of need, her body already aroused, hot and wet, just by the sight of him.

"Beautiful." Orin moved up and kissed Rekk's mouth, taking his time, giving the other man everything. Mya shucked off her clothes as she watched the intimate mating of mouths. Orin reached down and wrapped a hand around Rekk's cock rubbing him in time to his deep, thrusting kisses.

"*Mya.*"

Rekk was in her head, and so was Orin, making the experience of watching them kiss doubly erotic when she could also sense their feelings. And Gods, they both wanted it—wanted each other as much as they wanted her.

Rekk's hand grazed her hip and slid down, coming to rest with his palm upward, cupping her wet heat, his thumb wedged against her clit. She came so fast she bent over with the pleasure, grasping Rekk's shoulder as she panted out his name. Orin's fingers curved over her breast, tugging at her nipple, making her widen her legs to capture every slide of Rekk's still-working fingers.

She gasped as Rekk lifted her in one easy motion, setting her over his face while Orin moved down to attend to Rekk's cock. Rekk's tongue flicked and circled her already pulsing clit, and she rolled her hips, shoving herself down on him. Her second climax was even better than the first.

"I want... you both," Rekk managed to say. "With me right now."

"Not a problem." Orin said. "Sit up, Rekk, with your back against the tree."

She was lifted again, turned and slowly lowered over Rekk's big cock. She rocked back and forth, taking him inch-by-inch, aware of both men watching her progress, eager to proceed but enjoying the show anyway.

"Nice," Orin murmured. He sucked her nipple into his mouth and then kissed his way down to her cunt and licked her clit making her come and Rekk hiss a curse.

"I want my cock in your ass so bad, Rekk, but I don't want to hurt you."

"I don't care." Rekk lifted his head to gaze at Orin. "I want you there."

"But—"

"Please. Let me make my own choices. Don't make them for me."

Mya grabbed Orin's arm. "Oil in my backpack, for the cooking pot."

Orin made a face. "Better than nothing? Be right back."

Mya returned her full attention to Rekk who was smiling up at her.

"Would you rather be on top?" she asked. "I forgot how much you hate being held down."

"Not by you." His gaze narrowed as he rolled his hips. "With you, everything feels good and right."

"But if you want Orin…"

"I'm going to have to move." His hands rested on her hips, holding her down hard on his thick length. "But let me enjoy the view for a moment longer."

She dropped her shoulder so that her breast swung close to his face. With a stifled sound, he took her offering, drawing her into his mouth, sending a sharp pang of need straight to her sex that almost made her cry out.

He rolled her onto her back and pounded into her, each slam of his hips a reminder of his strength and size. She wrapped her thighs high around his torso and clung to him, angling her sex to take full advantage of every thrust.

When she opened her eyes after her third shattering climax, Orin loomed over Rekk's shoulder, and from the expression on his face, he was already probing Rekk's ass.

"Tight and nice," he murmured. "Just how I like them."

Rekk groaned. "Take me. Fuck me, don't... play with me."

Orin bit his shoulder. "Don't worry, I'll take you, big man. I've been waiting for this moment for a while, so I'm going to make the most of it."

Rekk stayed deep inside Mya and held still, his gaze tightening as Orin eased himself inside. "That is... Gods," he breathed out hard. "*Perfect.*"

"Yeah?" Orin wrapped one strong arm around both Rekk and Mya. "I haven't even started yet."

And then it was all about the sharing of flesh and pleasure and the melding of minds into one mass of overwhelming sensations. Mya closed her eyes and just held on, letting the enormity of the union wash over and through her. If she had doubted Rekk belonged with them before, she was now certain she'd been wrong. He fitted with them perfectly. Gods, what if they lost him after having experienced *this*?

Above her Rekk groaned. "I need to come... *I need.*"

Orin muttered something indecipherable and fucked harder, his weight pushing Rekk deeper into Mya. Not that she minded —this was everything she had ever dreamed a mated Triad could be and nothing like she had feared.

She climaxed, and, with a shout, Rekk joined her, followed almost instantly by Orin. For a long moment there was no sound but their harried breathing and thumping hearts. Their limbs were all tangled together, and Mya was on the bottom. She shoved at Orin's shoulder.

"Move."

He rolled over to one side, and Rekk rolled to the other, leaving her flat on her back as if she were completely winded. She pointed vaguely to her left.

"There's a stream over there. The water is quite warm."

With a chuckle, Rekk bent and picked her up in his arms.

"Let me help you up."

She buried her face in his shoulder and just breathed in the smell of sex and sweat. It was so good she wanted to lick him clean. He brought her to the stream and kept walking until he was up to his knees before he gently set her down. Luckily, he kept hold of her because her knees immediately buckled.

Behind them Orin cursed as he waded into the stream and immediately sank down to his knees. "It's freezing."

"It's warm enough," Rekk said as Mya lowered herself into the water. "You are obviously not used to living in the wilds."

"I'm a city boy. I want a hot shower and a large bed so I can go to sleep with you two."

"Tomorrow," Mya said and then looked away. "I mean if…"

"If I still want you both?" Rekk asked. He looked at Orin and then at her. "Do you still doubt that?"

"It's not that simple." Mya smoothed her fingers over his chest. "You need to find out who you are. You might already be *mated* for all we know."

"Do you not think I would remember that?" Rekk hesitated. "But maybe not. I think the Etruscans erased parts of my memory to prevent me from trying to escape again." His mouth twisted. "They seemed to believe I would forget my homeland and grow content to be a laboratory rat."

Mya splashed water over herself and shivered. "You are free now."

"Thanks to you. Whatever happens tomorrow, Mya, I will never forget that."

Orin stood and turned toward the bank, as if he couldn't bear to contribute anything to a conversation regarding Rekk leaving. "Let's get some sleep."

10

HE WAS AFRAID AGAIN. THE TEMPLE PROVED REASSURINGLY THE same, but it was also different. Torches had been replaced with powered lights and solar panels, and the people attending the ceremonies looked nothing like those he remembered.

Rekk's gaze dropped to Mya and Orin, who stood on either side of him. As soon as their party had arrived at the main gates, a priestess had met them and taken them directly through to the private-audience chamber the Oracle used for special guests. They'd had to give up their weapons, and he knew they hated that

The doors opened, and a tall woman he didn't recognize nodded a cool greeting.

"Welcome. The Oracle will see you now."

Rekk turned to Orin and Mya. "I wish to meet her alone. Will you wait here for me?"

Orin nodded immediately. Mya looked as if she wanted to protest, but obviously thought better of it.

He moved forward into the small, high-ceilinged room. At one end, there was a modest throne set on a dais. At the other was a table and chairs. The woman led him toward the table.

115

"Please be seated. I'll ask for some refreshments to be brought to you."

Just as Rekk pulled out a chair, a breeze blew the scent of exotic flowers toward him, and he turned toward the inner door.

"Rekk Pavan? It is you!"

The name resonated through his chest and settled there like an unyielding rock of truth.

"Oracle." He went to kneel, but she had already reached him and grabbed his hands.

"I always prayed you would return. I never gave up hope."

She was still beautiful, but older than he'd anticipated, and yet he knew her life span was three or four times that of an average Pavlovan. The Etruscans had obviously not allowed him to age as he should have done.

"Have my family been informed of my return?"

She cupped his chin, her gaze full of sorrow and compassion. "You have been away for quite some time, my friend."

"My mother? My sister?"

"They are both dead."

He took a moment to allow that to sink in. "Then who is left?"

"Just me."

"I don't...understand."

"Rekk, you were away for over a hundred years."

Silence fell between them. Had Mya and Orin known this? He would deal with that hurt later. All his attention was required to make sense of the enormity of what the Oracle was telling him.

"You know I would not lie to you."

"Yes, Oracle." In his heart he'd guessed something was terribly wrong and chosen to ignore it. His years of daring to hope were long past.

"The members of the Senate asked if I would be willing to

meet with you and identify you when they could not." She took his hand and made him sit down beside her at the table. "They couldn't believe the evidence before their own eyes."

"And you remember me?"

"Of course. There was some talk of us being mated at one point, although we had already decided we would be better off as friends." Her smile was wistful. "We were both being groomed for challenging roles. I think we found solace in each other over the demands we were constantly being subjected to."

"I hated my life." It was all coming back to him—as if the Oracle's mere presence had regenerated his memories. "I never wanted to follow in my father's footsteps."

"I remember. He died far too young, and you were thrust into a difficult situation." She smiled at him. "One thing you *might* like about this new world of ours is that the Pavlovan First Families gave the authority to govern over to the Senate, which means you can choose to be a private citizen or offer your valuable expertise to the assembly, but only if you wish."

"What valuable experience?" He looked away. "I was held captive by the Etruscans. They treated me as a cross between a science experiment and a prostitute."

"I heard something of this." Her face softened. "I am so sorry, Rekk."

He sprang up from his chair and paced back and forth in front of the long windows. Anger rolled inside him like the beginnings of a storm. "Why didn't anyone try to find me?"

"They did try—until a reliable Etruscan source showed your family evidence that the ship you escaped on crashed on one of their moons and that there were no survivors."

"That source was incorrect." He forced a laugh. "It was a miracle I was found at all, wasn't it?"

"Not quite." She hesitated. "I had a dream about you. I insisted that Captain Jong was to be part of the military delegation to the Etruscan moon."

Rekk pivoted around. "You *sent* her to find me?"

She shrugged. "That's what the Gods told me to do."

"Did she know beforehand?"

"I have no idea; you'll have to ask her."

"I will. Have I your permission to leave this place?"

"As long as you stay within the Temple grounds you may roam where you will. I do however expect to see you in my private apartments for dinner tonight so that we can talk more about your future." She stood up and took his hand. "Tread softly, my friend. I understand that this is difficult for you, but do not rush to any conclusions."

"One thing I learned during my captivity was patience. I am no longer that foolish boy who ran away rather than face up to his responsibilities."

She stroked his cheek. "You were never foolish, my dear, just unhappy about the hand fate dealt you. Think of this as an opportunity to rewrite your fate, and all will be well."

Greatly daring, he kissed her cheek. "Thank you for being honest with me, Oracle."

"I have no choice in that. I merely channel the Gods."

"So you accepted your fate as I have never been able to accept mine."

"I… grew into my power and discovered I rather liked it."

She surprised a smile out of him. He doubted many people saw this side of the all-powerful Oracle, decider of fates and mates and the future of their race.

"I don't know what to do," he confessed.

She patted his arm. "Then do nothing. You are most welcome to stay here for as long as you need."

"Are all my family gone?"

"You have some relatives from the other founding families. The current leader of the Senate, Ash, is the grandson of your mother's brother."

"I would like to meet him."

"I suspect he would like to meet you, too. Despite what you think, you still carry princely blood in your veins and have had experiences that none here can match. You also have enormous telepathic power, something that has been declining in our population for years. Mayhap you can help us recover that." She stepped back. "Now go and do what you must. I've asked my daughter to assign you a room in my private wing. She will take you there when you are ready."

"Thank you again."

Her smile was beautiful. "Don't thank me. Do you have any idea how wonderful it is for me to find my childhood friend again? Almost everyone I grew up with has died."

He bowed low. "Then we are doubly blessed to have each other."

He backed out of the room and turned as Mya and Orin both jumped to their feet.

"Are you okay?" Mya asked. "Was the Oracle able to tell you who you are?"

"Yes. Did you know?"

"Know what?"

"That I'd been held captive for over a hundred years? That I am a hundred and twenty-five years old and my family are all dead?"

She didn't have to speak the words out loud; he felt her answer in his mind.

"You did know, but you chose not to tell me."

"I was under orders not to reveal anything to you that might cause you further suffering."

He stepped in close and lowered his voice. "You would keep such things from a male you insist is your *mate*?"

"That's not fair, Rekk. I took on this assignment in good faith. I had no ability to communicate with my superiors or ask them to change the parameters of that mission."

"How convenient."

Orin cleared his throat. "Rekk, we know you're angry, but—"

He rounded on the other male. "You have *no idea* how I feel. *You* are not the person who has been lied to by the two people who are supposed to have his best interests at heart!"

Orin frowned. "Hey, you were the one saying those ties didn't exist. You can't have it both ways."

"Obviously." He glared at Orin. "Did you also know I was a prince of the blood?"

"I don't even know what the heeze that means."

"I knew," Mya said. She faced Rekk. "That's one of the reasons why I was reluctant to believe you truly could be our Third."

"Even though you were specifically selected for the mission to bring me back?"

"*What?*" Mya went still. "That was *not* our purpose."

He found himself glaring at her. "You were sent to bring me back. Mayhap you decided it would be worth the risk to secure a prince?"

"That's not true! I was *sent* because I am the best member of my team. I had no idea that you were there!" She squared up to him. "Or are you suggesting I was *used*? That they deliberately set me up to be taken and drugged and..."

"Forced to have sex with me?" Rekk finished for her. "Maybe it's all been a big lie, Mya. Maybe we've both been used and there really is nothing between us after all."

He turned and walked away, his feet unconsciously following a path down to one of the secluded gardens where he'd played so happily as a child. He couldn't bear to deal with anyone else at this moment. He needed time to understand the chaos his life had suddenly become.

"Damn." Orin shoved a hand through his hair. "That didn't go well."

Mya forced her limbs to stop trembling. "He behaved *appallingly*!"

"Mya, the guy just found out that's he's a hundred and twenty-five years old, his family are all dead, and he's the heir to a kingdom that no longer exists! Give him some space."

"Like he gave us? Insinuating that we lied to him and used him, suggesting that I wasn't given that job because I'm the best there is, but because he would be *attracted* to me?"

"Hold up. If you were sent on that mission for reasons other than the usual, that was hardly Rekk's fault. He was stuck in captivity. I doubt he was able to direct what happened from there."

Mya took a deep breath. "Okay. I'll give you that, but he suggested I *knew*, and I sure as heeze did not."

"You knew all the other stuff, so why wouldn't he think you knew that as well?"

Mya flung out her hand. "Shut *up*, Orin."

"Talk to Major Esca about what went down." Orin hesitated. "Rekk's a big deal, Mya. I suspect if they wanted him back they would use anyone to get him."

Mya walked over to the door and opened it to reveal one of the priestesses waiting patiently outside. She refused to give in to her emotions just yet. She was better than that—she was *stronger*. "Do you have somewhere I can place a secure call through to the military?"

"You would need to speak to Captain Ian McNeill, our head of security. Would you like me to take you to his offices?"

A KEEN-EYED MAN leaned over the security desk, checking some detail on one of the exterior cameras. He straightened. "Can I help you?"

His accent was unfamiliar, but he was as military as they came, his blue gaze watchful as Mya and Orin were escorted into his domain.

Mya fought the temptation to salute. "I wish to speak with my commanding officer, Major Esca, about the completion of my mission. I understand you can provide us with a secure channel."

"You brought Rekk Pavan in, didn't you? Nice work."

"Thank you." Mya didn't smile.

"Roberts told me you would succeed."

"You know Lieutenant Roberts?"

"Yeah." Captain McNeill walked them through a couple rooms and entered a secure code at the next door. "We came from Earth together with my mate, the future Oracle." He held the door open and stood aside. "Here you go. I've already added you both to our secure roster. Just go ahead and key in your codes, and you should be fine."

"Thank you."

"You're welcome. When you've finished, I'd appreciate your feedback on the Etruscans you dealt with on the way here."

"We'd be delighted to help with that."

Orin glanced over at Mya as he shut the door. "How in the Gods' name did an earthling end up mated to the Oracle's heir?"

Mya shrugged. "I have no idea. It's almost as ridiculous as us thinking we meant something to Rekk Pavan, isn't it?"

Orin wisely didn't say anything to that and took a seat, familiarizing himself with the control panel.

"You go first," she offered.

He bowed. "No, after you. I'm dying to hear how you're going to deal with this one, my mate."

Mya keyed in a series of codes and within seconds, Major

Esca appeared on the screen. His smile widened as he took in Mya's face.

"Congratulations, you made it. We were getting worried when your whole security team got blown up, but I knew you'd get through."

"I'll send you a full report of our journey, sir, as soon as I've recorded it."

"Good. Did the Oracle recognize our man?"

"Yes, sir. She did."

Major Esca sat back. "That's amazing. He's really over a hundred years old?"

"Apparently so." Mya took a quick breath. "Sir, can you confirm whether the military knew of Rekk Pavan's presence on the Etruscan moon?"

"Not that I know of, why?"

"Because I've been led to believe that I was specifically selected to go on the mission in order to find him and... mate with him."

Major Esca sat forward. "Hold on a moment. What are you trying to say?"

She forced herself to ask the question. "Did you intentionally send me on that mission knowing what would happen to me?"

"Captain Jong, if you think I am the kind of commanding officer who would do that, you don't know me at all." All traces of amusement were stripped from his face.

"I didn't think you would, sir."

"But you believe someone did? Will you trust me to investigate this matter further and get back to you as soon as I can?"

"Yes, sir."

"If you were deliberately sent into that situation... I'll personally get hold of whoever gave that order and rip his head off."

"Thank you, sir."

"You're welcome. Esca out."

The screen went blue again, as if her superior officer had leapt out of his chair to go and find the answers. Knowing him as she did, it was highly likely.

She let out a slow breath. So if Major Esca hadn't deliberately set her up, who had? Unless Rekk was lying to her as well… She didn't want to think about him. Sure, he had a right to be angry that he hadn't been given all the facts, but she'd done the best she could in the circumstances. It wasn't her fault that she'd fallen in love with her damaged hero.

Orin spoke to Lieutenant Roberts and checked in with his precinct boss, receiving a host of typically off-color police jokes from his comrades, which didn't bother him at all. Was he upset about Rekk? He didn't seem to be, but then he wasn't the one who'd been dragged through hell to save a prince.

"Yeah, right back at you, bunch of losers." Orin signed off and turned to Mya, his grin fading. "You okay?"

"Not really." She hunched a shoulder. "Maybe I'll feel better after a shower and a nap."

"While you were talking to Major Esca we were invited to have dinner with the Oracle—and when I say invited, I mean commanded, so we have to go."

Mya groaned. "Do you think Rekk will be there as well?"

"I would imagine so." Orin gave her the side eye. "Don't you want to see him?"

"Do you?"

"Sure I do."

"Even though he thinks we're both liars?"

"He doesn't really think that. He's just angry at everything at the moment, and we're the most obvious targets."

Mya put her hands on her hips. "How did you work that out?"

"Because he knows we care about him and we'll forgive him?"

"You're some kind of philosopher now?" She raised her chin.

"I'm not sure about that, and I'm not committing to *anything* until I hear whether what he said was true."

"You can't blame him if the military set up this whole thing, Mya."

She raised an eyebrow. "You're on his side now?"

"I'm not taking sides. He's in shock because his whole world has changed, and he's struggling to trust anyone. *You're* in shock because you've discovered you might have been used as bait. Unfortunately, you're both blaming the messenger, but they are two very separate issues."

"I don't like it when you get all sensible on me."

"Wow, Hakron pride sure is thorny." Orin held up his hands in surrender. "Fair enough, but you're going to have to be polite and sit through dinner, okay?"

"If I must." Mya rose from her chair and opened the door. "Let's go and find our quarters."

11

Rekk stared at the variety of garments someone had laid out on his bed while he'd been in the shower. There were his newly washed jeans and T-shirt, a white robe with a sash that he guessed belonged to the Oracle's bodyguard, and a swathe of gold silk that shimmered in the light. There was a breeze, but it was still a warm evening. What should he choose? The traditional Temple attire, his now much-loved jeans, or the draped silk of a prince?

He picked up the silk and smoothed it with his thumb. It was shot through with a fine gold thread. Was it some kind of test? That by choosing one set of clothes, he was somehow committing to a particular identity?

His family was dead. His nearest living relative was a hundred years younger than him, his status in society had changed dramatically, and he'd managed to offend the two people who'd saved his life and brought him safely home.

With a groan, Rekk covered his face with his hands. It didn't stop him seeing Mya's expression as he'd laid into her about her lack of trust, her shock when he'd insisted that she'd been sent after him deliberately. She hadn't deserved his anger, but he'd felt so raw, so betrayed by everyone he had ever cared about...

He opened his eyes. Hadn't he wanted Mya and Orin to see him as he was? The Oracle had promised him she could strengthen his shields and retrain his telepathic abilities, but that it would take some time. Did he *have* time? He couldn't return to the past. Did he want to become a different man?

It seemed he had no choice. He couldn't go on as he was. Rising to his feet, he made his choice of clothing and headed out to dinner with the Oracle.

ORIN GLANCED SURREPTITIOUSLY around the table. Rekk wasn't there yet, but he was expected. How the heeze had he ended up eating dinner with the Oracle of Pavlovan, her eldest daughter, and her two mates? He was just a simple man. Mya was quiet, but he suspected that was more because she was worrying about what Major Esca would have to tell her than because she was overawed.

"Thank you for bring Rekk safely home, Orin Mazak."

He swallowed down his drink, almost choked, and turned to the Oracle who was sitting on his left. For a woman of well over a hundred years of age, she looked remarkably youthful.

"It was our pleasure, Goddess on Earth."

She leaned forward until her lips were almost touching his ear. Her power shimmered through him and he worried he might lose it big time.

"Your mate seems distracted this evening. Is she all right?"

"She's waiting on some information from Major Esca about our mission."

"Ah."

Her thought pierced his mind with the clarity of a bell. *"She doubts that Rekk is also her mate?"*

"Uh…"

"I sent her to find him. I knew she was the only one who could save his life. He'd given up. I could sense his life force failing."

"You sent her?" Too late Orin realized he'd spoken out loud.

Mya looked up, her gaze shifting from him to the Oracle, her expression formidable.

The Oracle smiled sweetly. "Yes, indeed. I had a vision."

"Then it wasn't a military decision after all?" Mya asked.

"I don't know about that, my dear. I merely made the suggestion that—"

Mya rose slowly to her feet and all conversation at the table abruptly halted. Captain O'Neill tensed as if ready to throw himself in front of the Oracle.

"You sent me there as bait so that you could recover a prince of the blood?"

"Um… Mya." Orin looked from her to the Oracle. "Don't you think you should—"

"Shut up, Orin." Maya glared at the Oracle. "How *could* you?"

"How could I send you to find your Third and bring him home? How could I *not?*" The Oracle rose too, her power growing to encompass the whole room. "I knew you and Orin were coming to the Temple to find your Third. Then I had a vision, and I knew you had to go to that Etruscan moon first."

"I almost died there. We *both* almost died."

"But you didn't." The Oracle held her gaze. "I knew you wouldn't, otherwise I would never have sent you. Are you suggesting that your sacrifice wasn't worth it? Don't you want a Third?"

A flash of gold at the dining room door drew Orin's attention to the man draped in gold silk who stood quietly listening to the heated discussion. Rekk looked like some kind of god in the glinting fabric that matched his eyes and made Orin long to rip it off him and—

"Mya."

He tried to warn her, but she was too focused on the Oracle to hear him.

"You risked our lives, you risked *Orin's* life just to see your vision come to fruition?"

"I am the Oracle. Why would I not?" The goddess raised her chin. "I channel the desires of the Gods. I do their will. I do not question their wisdom."

"But what if you're wrong? What if Rekk doesn't believe we are mated? Was it all a mistake *then?*"

"You question the will of the Gods?"

Icy power poured through the Oracle's voice, making Orin and everyone else around the table shiver.

"Mya. Sit down, okay?" Orin muttered and grabbed her hand. "This isn't going to end well."

She took a deep breath. "I'm sorry if I offended you, Oracle. I'm just… confused."

"Understandably. It is hard even for me to interpret the desires of the Gods sometimes, and I've been doing this for over a hundred years." The Oracle glanced at the doorway. "Perhaps you might care to explain to Rekk why your journey to find him was unnecessary."

"I didn't say that." Mya turned toward Rekk. "I am *glad* he was returned safely to his people. No one deserves to be held and used like that."

He bowed. "Thank you, Captain Jong. I, too, wish that you and your mate had not been dragged into danger merely to keep me alive."

He advanced slowly into the room, his bare feet making no sound on the paved floor. "I also apologize for any assumptions I might have made about your character." He paused, his gaze fixed on Mya. "You deserve only my thanks."

She nodded once as Rekk turned his attention to Orin.

"Thank you, as well."

Orin grinned at him. "You're welcome."

The Oracle clapped her hands. "If we have finished discussing this fascinating subject, might we all sit down and finish our dinner? Rekk, you may sit on my right."

He sat down, the silk fabric settling easily around his body. Orin could get nothing from Rekk's mind. Either the Oracle was shielding for him, or he was already getting to grips with his powers. Orin's appetite died. He didn't want to be shut out from that power. He wanted to be surrounded by it, bathed in it, *part* of it.

"So you're done with me?" Orin asked.

Rekk's hand fisted on the table. *"I am trying to protect you."*

"Do you feel better hiding behind those shields?"

"No."

And then there was nothing but a wall of steel. Orin started to eat again, chewing determinedly at each delicacy presented to him, determined to enjoy the experience even if it killed him. What the heeze was Rekk playing at?

"He's giving you space to think."

That was Mya. Orin checked out her stiff posture and closed-in expression.

"Now you're on his side? I don't want to be given anything let alone space."

"But maybe he does. We can't force him to acknowledge us. It has to be up to him."

"I'm sure I could persuade him if you let me."

Mya rolled her eyes at him, and he took the hint. At least he and Mya had each other. Rekk was dealing with a whole new world.

"Why won't he let us help him?"

"Orin... sometimes we have to work things out for ourselves."

"Like me not killing Rekk when I first found him with you?"

"Something like that."

"I don't like this at all." Orin cut into his meat and glowered

across the table at Rekk, who was conversing with the Oracle. *"I'm going to take a piss."*

After making his excuses, he stomped down the hallway to the swankiest bathroom he'd ever been in. He took his time striving to find his patient side and failed miserably. He walked out into the hallway and immediately collided with someone. His hand flattened on a muscular chest and expensive silk.

"I beg your pardon, Orin, I did not realize…"

Within a second, Orin had his mouth on Rekk's and his body slammed up against the wall while he kissed him. Not that Rekk seemed to want to get away; he was kissing him back just as enthusiastically.

Orin drew away, panting.

"Just so you don't forget what you're missing while you're doing all this thinking, okay?"

Rekk nodded as if still in a daze as Orin forced himself to peel away from Rekk and return to the dining room. Mya would kill him, but he'd had to take a stand and make the other male notice him. Make Rekk realize that he was still wanted even though he was a goddammned prince.

"Yeah, like he needs me," Orin muttered even as he acknowledged that if Rekk didn't want him, he'd be gutted.

Mya glanced up as he sat down. "Everything all right?"

"All good." His plate had been removed and the table was now covered in dessert, which was his favorite thing. He knew he had it bad when even that couldn't make him feel better.

"Mya, do you still want Rekk?"

Mya waited so long to answer him that he thought she never would. *"Yes, but—"*

"No buts. This is a simple question."

"But it isn't simple, is it? We have to give him some time. I realize that now."

"I still don't like it."

"Neither do I." She smiled at him. *"But we're going to do this*

right, okay? I can't deal with establishing a Triad where one member gets coerced into joining. I want it all done by consent and properly sanctified by the Oracle."

"Very wise." The Oracle broke into their supposedly private link. *"He is not ready yet. Give him the gift of time and understanding."*

<hr>

MYA WAITED until Rekk returned to his seat opposite her and then leaned forward to talk to him. He looked like something out of an old painting with his golden robes and distant, courteous expression.

"May we speak with you after dinner?"

"Yes, of course."

His mind was guarded against her, and very little of his immense power flowed through her. Somehow it made it easier for her to recognize the strength of her own yearnings and her own needs.

She still wanted him. The revelation settled over her and she accepted it in her soul. As she'd said to Orin, she would never force Rekk to make a decision about their mating, but she would no longer pretend she didn't want him in her life and in her Triad.

After the dinner ended, she, Orin, and Rekk were shown into a small private room adjoining the courtyard that looked down over the bulk of the Temple buildings. The smell of incense and flowers rose from the chanting crowds below, giving the space an almost ethereal atmosphere.

None of them sat down, but Orin arranged himself at Mya's side, his hand on her shoulder, which gave her much needed comfort. She started to speak, but Rekk held up his hand.

"Let me start by apologizing again. I did not behave well

when we last met. I was still reeling from all the shocks. I felt betrayed—especially by you—which was unfair."

"But understandable," Mya said. "I apologize for keeping things from you."

"Which she only did because she was under strict orders from her superiors," Orin chimed in.

"I understand that now." Rekk nodded. "I cannot believe that someone deliberately sent you to find me. Did you discover who it was?"

"The Oracle said she told someone about her vision— presumably someone whom she believed could make sure I was *sent* on that mission. It wasn't my immediate boss. He's looking into it for me."

Rekk shoved a hand through his hair. "I would rather have stayed in captivity than have them risk your life to save mine. On my honor."

"Yeah," Orin said. "I'd probably feel the same."

"You are too... important to me," Rekk carried on speaking, his gaze locked with Mya's.

"I am?" A sudden hope filled her heart. She wanted to make him admit his feelings, to force him to say more, but she held back. "The Oracle said she would not have sent me to find you unless I'd been capable of bringing you safely home."

"She should not have taken it upon herself to make that deci-sion." Rekk looked fierce. "She is not infallible and neither are her visions. You still might have been killed."

Silence fell and Mya waited to hear if Rekk had more to say before she gathered her courage and took Orin's hand.

"We wanted to tell you that we still wish to have you in our lives, and that we respect your need for time to think through this very difficult episode of your life. If after a period of sepa-ration, you decide that you would like to see us again, I'm sure the Oracle would be more than willing to contact us."

Rekk went still. "You're both leaving?"

Beside her Orin cleared his throat. "Yeah, we're giving you some space, okay? Just like you asked."

Mya gripped his hand so hard she thought she might have broken something. "We want you, but we won't force you into anything. You don't deserve that. You deserve to enjoy your new freedom and the ability to make your own decisions for a while."

"That is very… kind of you both."

"It's the only thing we can do." Mya's voice trembled. "We wish you nothing but the best, and we will be thinking about you every single day." She swallowed hard. "If you realize you don't need us anymore? Then let us know, and we will still wish you all the best in your new life."

She walked out, dragging Orin with her, and practically ran all the way up the stairs to their shared bedroom. Orin only paused to lock the door before gathering her in his arms and letting her cry.

After a long while she managed to look up at him. "I feel as if I've made a terrible mistake."

"You haven't. You were incredibly brave." He kissed her nose. "You're right. We have to let him choose for all our sakes."

"But it hurts," she whispered and pressed a hand to her chest. "Right here."

"I know, love. Heeze, I know…"

"Thank you for coming, Captain Jong, Lieutenant Mazak."

Major Esca ushered them both into the office that would soon be Mya's—if she took the promotion she'd been offered the previous week. She still hadn't made up her mind. It had been almost a month since they'd left the Temple and returned to the capital city. Orin had returned to work, and Mya's unit had been settled at their home base doing various boring training courses.

She immediately saluted as she spotted Senator Ash seated at his Second Male's desk. He still looked tired, his almost white hair tied back from his angular face, but he was no longer in danger from the head wound that had threatened his life.

"Senator Ash." They both bowed respectfully.

"Please sit down, Captain Jong, and you, too, Lieutenant Mazak. This meeting will be in confidence, off record and confidential."

"Yes, sir."

Major Esca took a chair to the side of his desk and nodded at the Senator to go on.

"First of all, the Senate thanks you both for your

outstanding work in bringing back Rekk Pavan. We cannot 'officially' thank you because the matter is not public, nor do we want it to be. "

Both Mya and Orin nodded.

"Secondly, I wanted to address the accusation that Captain Jong was deliberately selected to go on this mission." Senator Ash sat forward. "Even though Major Esca was unaware of this, there was some… external pressure applied to ensure you went, Captain."

"I understand that the Oracle had a vision." Mya attempted to sound neutral. "Was that pressure applied by her?"

"She did speak to a small group of senators. One of them might have used his influence to make certain you were included in that team."

"Even though I was intending to send you anyway, because you were the best person for the job," Major Esca added.

Mya frowned. "They caught me within a few minutes of our landing craft touching down. I did wonder at the time whether someone had known we were coming."

"And that's the interesting part. For some time, we've had a sense that someone high up in our government is working with the Etruscans to bring us down. The person who informed the Etruscans about your arrival, and your potential impact on their prisoner, must have hoped you would be captured and never heard of again."

"But we escaped."

"As the Oracle predicted." Senator Ash nodded. "And now we know for certain that someone is betraying us, and we have been able to narrow the possibilities down to about five members of the Assembly. So you have done us a double service, Captain."

"Why would any Pavlovan traitor care about Mya and Rekk?" Orin asked.

"Because Rekk is the last survivor of the original founding

families. His grandfather was one of the first to colonize our planet. His family used to rule this world."

"So?"

"So he could have been used as a rallying point—a true prince of the blood—and if he had stayed in Etruscan hands they could've used him against us."

"Poor Rekk," Mya murmured.

"But we don't have a monarchy. We have a senate," Orin persisted. "Rekk belongs to an outmoded system."

"True, but there are always those who harken back to the old days and would be willing to use any grievance against the current senate to power a revolution."

"Especially if the Etruscans were whipping up the flames." Orin nodded. "I get it now."

"But does Rekk *want* to take over the senate?" Mya found herself asking the question despite herself.

"If the Etruscans still had him, I don't think he would have had much of a choice, do you? They were deliberately eroding his defenses and making him forget his true identity. The fact that he fought them for so long truly shows his amazing spirit and loyalty to his nation."

"And yet he thinks he is worth nothing," Mya said quietly. "What will happen to him now?"

Major Esca stood up and went to the door. "Maybe you should ask him yourself."

Rekk came through the door. He wore the jeans and grey T-shirt she'd bought him on their journey to the Temple and had allowed his hair to grow a little longer. Beside her Orin made a purring sound, as though he'd just spotted his favorite dessert.

"Do you wish to take over the planet, Rekk Pavan?" Major Esca asked.

"No, thank you." Rekk's gaze swept over Mya and Orin. "I'd much rather live a quiet life somewhere with people I love."

Senator Ash rose with some difficulty from his chair. "I

think that's our cue to leave, Esca." He winked at Orin and Mya. "I wish you both well, and congratulations on finding your Third."

"We haven't—"

Mya elbowed Orin hard in the ribs. "Thank you for everything, Senator Ash."

He paused and took a scroll out of his pocket. "I almost forgot. The Oracle asked me to give you this."

He left with Major Esca, closing the door firmly behind him, leaving a pool of silence.

Rekk moved to sit on the edge of the desk. "What does the Oracle have to say for herself?"

Mya untied the ribbon and released the scroll of paper.

"Shall I read it out loud?"

"Only if it's good news," Orin said.

"It's an official proclamation that Rekk is our Third." She lifted her gaze to Rekk's. "Did you know about this?"

"I did."

"And you accept it?"

He shrugged, his smile half hopeful and half scared. "If you both want me. I've had plenty of time to think, and all I could think of was being with you two." He went down on both knees. "Will you accept me as your Third?"

Joy flooded through Mya, followed by a wave of love that encompassed all three of them. "Yes, please."

Orin grinned down at Rekk. "Totally. And, while you're down there…"

Mya slapped his arm. "Behave yourself."

"I am. If we weren't in your boss's office, I'd had stripped him naked by now and fucked his brains out."

Rekk groaned and rose to his feet. "Don't say that."

Mya took his hand. "We do want you, but we will be going to the Temple to have an official ceremony. So you still have one more opportunity to change your mind."

He brought her fingers to his lips. "Generous of you. I've been working hard on my shields. I think I will be able to function normally in society now."

"Not with us. We want all that power."

"It is yours, as I am yours."

Orin wrapped an arm around both of them and drew them in for a group hug.

"I think we should go back home and celebrate—we are allowed to do that before the official ceremony aren't we?"

Rekk smiled. "I was hoping you would say that—seeing as I didn't book a hotel room for myself."

Orin snorted. "Typical royalty, always leeching off the poor."

Mya smiled at both her males. "Let's go. Last one to get naked has to watch." She turned and ran for the door, listening to the howls of outrage behind her as she sprinted down the stairs.

Life was good. Her Triad would be founded on rock and she was one very lucky female...

The End

A NOTE TO READERS

Dear Readers,

In book 5 of the Triad series you met Captain Mya Jong, a Hakron soldier who works with Major Esca. Her life got extremely complicated when her First Male suddenly wanted to find their Third and start a family. She was not thrilled by the idea, but that was before she was trapped on a hostile moon with a Telepath of incredible power...

If you enjoyed this book, please consider leaving a review at your favorite retailer.

If you want to read more of my books, please check out my website and consider joining my newsletter for the fastest updates and early contests to win new books.

katepearce.com/newsletter

Thank you for reading!
Kate Pearce

Continue the series with *Triad*...

Chapter One

Quoxor Province, Pavlovan

Rain Datta eased her heavy kit bag over her shoulder and approached the ticket booth, sliding her I.D. card across the counter.

"Good morning." Rain said politely.

The male leaned as far away as possible as he swiped her card.

"I need a ticket to the Neveks region in Quoxor Province," Rain continued. "I should have credits in place from the military. My number is—"

He pushed the card back using one fingertip. "I can't help you."

Rain frowned. "You do operate a service out there?"

"Yes." He glanced briefly at his screen. "Once a month. You just missed it."

"It was supposed to run today." Used to the vagaries of transportation outside the major cities, she tried again. "If I've missed the direct bus, there must be a way to get to Neveks using other routes, right?"

"Nothing that I can offer the likes of *you*."

His sneer this time was loud and obvious.

"Hang on a minute," Rain said, holding on to her temper by a thread. She'd already had a long day and was in no mood to make it worse. "Are you discriminating against me because I'm from Neveks? What *century* are we in?" She jabbed at her uniform. "I've served in the Pavlovan military!"

He still wouldn't look directly at her. "There's no point getting annoyed with me, female. I don't make the rules. Due to new regulations regarding native tribes in this region, I'm not allowed to sell you a ticket without prior authorization from my manager, your current employer, and the Neveks authorities. According to my systems your name isn't on *any* of those lists."

Rain let out a long slow breath. "This is *ridiculous*. What am I supposed to do now?"

The clerk shrugged.

"I'll buy her ticket."

The voice came from behind her, and she swung around to stare up at the unknown male. He was tall and had striking pale blue eyes and a hard face.

He nodded at her briefly, and then returned his cold gaze to the ticket seller. "No member of the Pavlovan military should be denied a seat on a public bus. I'll buy two tickets."

"You can't—"

"Get down!"

In a blur of motion, Rain was swept off her feet and rolled to the ground. From within the cradle of the man's arms, she watched as a large vehicle careered off the side of the road and came spinning down the bank toward the bus station, brakes squealing, horn blaring. It swung around in a slow, perfect arc, almost as if it was a vidmovie, and took out half the building as well as the two empty buses waiting for passengers to board.

"Wow." Rain breathed through a mouthful of dust.

There was a horrendous crashing and tearing of metal, and then everything shuddered to a stop. Rain pushed herself free and stood up, coughing in the smoke, and tried to assess the damage. It was early in the morning so there weren't many people around, and she could see no obvious casualties who needed help. She cautiously lowered her telepathic shields. No one appeared to be hurt.

The clerk leapt to his feet and pointed straight at Rain.

"You did this! You caused this, Thought Stealer, Mind Thief!"

Rain didn't bother to answer, but grabbed her pack, turned away, and headed out. It looked like she'd be walking, so she might as well get started before it got really ugly around there. Gradually the smoke and the dust settled behind her, and she breathed clean air. She could hear sirens and emergency vehicles and wondered whether the clerk would be dumb enough to send the authorities after her.

It wouldn't be the first time someone from Neveks was arrested for simply being in the wrong place at the wrong time.

"Hey."

She'd known someone was following her, so she wasn't surprised at the shout. It was a shame the military hadn't allowed her to bring her favorite weapon home, but she was trained in hand-to-hand combat so she could still hold her own. She didn't stop walking, but slowed enough to let the tall male come alongside her. It was the guy who'd offered to buy her a ticket and thrown her to the ground like a real hero.

"You still planning on going to Neveks?"

During her military service she'd met people from all over the planet, but his accent was unfamiliar and his mind…was like nothing she'd ever encountered before. She slowed down and faced him.

"Of course."

He studied her carefully. "How are you planning on getting there?"

"I've got these things." She pointed at her feet. "I'll walk."

"You don't want to share the cost of a rental?"

"A what?"

"A hired vehicle."

"No one in this town would rent me anything."

He raised an eyebrow. "Why's that?"

This time she stared at him for quite a while, but he didn't appear to be joking. "Because I'm from Neveks."

"The ticket guy called you a mind stealer. Does that have something to do with it?"

"Are you super slow or what?" She jabbed herself in the chest. "I'm from *Neveks*! We can read people's darkest thoughts and sub thoughts and bonded-Triad thoughts. Nothing is safe from our horrible, devious minds."

He regarded her impassively. "So what am I thinking right now?"

"You…are just weird." She started walking again.

"How?"

She spoke over her shoulder. "I don't have time to play games."

"I can't sense you in my head, so you're obviously not that powerful."

"You *can't*?"

He shrugged. "Nope. I have excellent shields."

"That usually doesn't matter." She stopped again. She

couldn't sense him, which was remarkably soothing. "You're not from around here, are you?"

"I'm from planet Earth."

She gave him her best don't-fuck-with-me look. "They don't have telepaths there, Earth man."

"It's hu-man, and let's just say it's an emerging talent." He hefted his backpack higher on his shoulder, his expression calm. "Are we walking or not?"

She shrugged, which Jay took for assent, and he fell in beside her. He could sense her in his head just fine, but as long as she wasn't aware of it, he was good.

"How long do you reckon it will take us to get to the Neveks region on foot?"

"A week if the weather stays fine and you don't hold me up." She didn't bother to look at him. "I know a few shortcuts off the main route."

"You've done this before?"

"You heard the man at the bus station. We're not popular, so most Neveks learn to have a backup plan."

"That sucks. I don't think I've met anyone from your region before."

That was the truth. The fact that he'd spent a month studying up on her culture, and all data available on her personally, was another matter entirely.

"That's because most of my people stay home." She sighed. "Which kind of makes anyone who *does* venture out into the world even more conspicuous and even less welcome. Why are you going to Neveks?"

"I'm actually heading for the Temple of Quoxor. I've got a big decision to make about my future, and that seemed like a good place to think it through." That was another truth. "I'm not particularly religious or anything, but your Oracle does seem to have some extraordinary powers. I've heard it's a great place to meditate, and I know one of the palace security team out there."

"She's not my Oracle. Neveks worship their own Queen Goddess who rules over our tribes."

"You don't go to the temple to find your Triad members?"

He knew most of this already, but he was trying to get her to trust him, and acting like the stranger in town was the best option available.

"No."

Damn. She sure wasn't chatty.

For a while she said nothing as they moved off the main highway and crossed into a wooded area. It was cooler under the trees and much quieter. He studied the unfamiliar trees and birds, his keen eye cataloguing each new sight and storing it in the A.I. database that masqueraded as his brain. Information came back to him, detailing which creatures were dangerous, which could be eaten, and which were poisonous.

He paused as a big blue bird laboriously flapped its way from one branch to another. His companion stopped as well, her face turned up to the filtered sunlight, her gaze everywhere. Her hair was black and tied at the nape of her neck, her eyes were as green as the foliage, and her skin…it was like watching a kaleidoscope in motion. Whatever she came near was reflected back in the changing shades of her melatonin.

"You're staring at me again," Rain said.

"I've never met someone from Neveks before." He shrugged. "You're like a chameleon."

"A what?"

"It's a creature we have on Earth that can change the color of its skin to avoid predators. I bet they loved having you in the military."

"They tolerated me." She smoothed a hand over her throat. "I had my uses. Are you military?"

It was only the second direct question she'd asked him. He wondered how much she could pick up despite his enhanced shields. It was one of the uncertainties about the Neveks telepathic reach he'd been directed to investigate.

"I was in the army on Earth. I was sent here with the Oracle's heir." He resumed walking and risked a question of his own. "Why are you going to Neveks?"

"My mother is ill. I've been given permission to visit her."

Jay pretended to consider her answer, even though he knew exactly where the permission had come from. "Why do you need an invitation? Aren't you going home?"

"I was kicked out when I was eighteen." This time her impatience showed on her face. "Can we keep walking? I'd like to be out of this wood before it gets dark."

"Sure, sorry. It's just nice to have someone to talk to, you know?" He glanced down at her unresponsive expression. "I've been traveling by myself for four weeks already."

She didn't ask him anything about his journey or himself, which was fine by him. He didn't like lying, and if she was prepared to tolerate him tagging along while he attempted to gain her trust and entry into Neveks? That was good enough for now.

"My name's Jay. What's yours?"

"Rain."

"Like the weather or like a queen?"

"The weather I suppose." She shrugged. "I didn't pick it."

"It's nice."

She gave him an eye-roll for that bit of pandering, and he stopped talking.

The scene at the transit center had been carefully staged to make her notice him being heroic. When the bus careered toward them, he'd relied on his enhanced hearing and speed to get her out of harm's way. Not that she'd acknowledged his derring-do. She'd simply stood up, brushed herself down, and disappeared in the crowd. He'd already guessed from the speed with which she'd vanished that she was pretty good at taking care of herself, but at least he'd managed some kind of an introduction.

He dug in his backpack for his water bottle and held it out. "You want some?"

"I've got my own, thanks."

He'd told her that he couldn't sense her thoughts, but that wasn't true. Like all telepaths on Pavlovan, she gave off a subtle signal that resonated with his enhanced senses. When he and the other guys had first arrived from Earth, the sound of that collective psychic energy had been a balm to their much-abused systems. It was only the second time in his life when he'd actually felt like he belonged somewhere.

"Do people from Neveks form Triads like the rest of Pavlovan?"

"Yeah."

"But without the help of the Oracle?"

She shifted the strap of her backpack onto her other shoulder. "The Queen Goddess makes the decisions."

"All of them?"

"Pretty much." She glanced up at the angle of the sun. "We should keep walking for another hour or so, and then stop to eat. It gets steeper from here in as we follow the path through the mountains."

"Which is your polite way of telling me to shut up and keep moving." He surprised a quick smile out of her, which she quickly covered with a frown. "Lead on. I'll try and keep up."

She increased her pace, and so did he. He could walk for days without stopping, but she didn't know that, and he didn't want to make her suspicious. He'd monitor her body for signs of fatigue and match whatever she did. It was possible that she might try and evade him for reasons of her own. No matter what happened, he was sticking to her like glue. She didn't know it yet, but the very future of planet Pavlovan might depend on it.

End of Sample

To continue reading, be sure to pick up Triad at your favorite retailer.

ALSO BY KATE PEARCE

The Diable Delamere Series
Historical Romance

Regency dukes, disinherited aristocrats and a plot to assassinate the Prince Regent create plenty of problems for all the heroes and heroines as they struggle to trust each other in an ever-changing game of love, deceit and treachery.

The Millcastle Series
Historical Romance

On the cusp of the industrial revolution in the northern town of Millcastle the old and the new clash both in matters of business and of the heart. Can love flourish among the rush to make a profit?

House of Pleasure / Simply Series
Historical Erotic Romance

Enter a Regency house of pleasure where nothing is forbidden and every sexual desire you have ever imagined can come true...

The Sinners Club

Historical Erotic Romance

When intrigue collides with heated passion behind the closed doors of the Sinners Club there is nowhere left to hide.

.

The Morgan Ranch Series

Contemporary Western Romance

A Northern Californian ranching family torn apart by tragedy reluctantly return home to discover not everything was as they thought it was, and that love, and forgiveness can sometimes go hand in hand.

.

The Millers of Morgan Valley Series

Contemporary Western Romance

When the mother you haven't seen for twenty years asks to visit your family ranch and set the record straight, how will her ex and six adult children react? The loves and sometimes messy lives of a ranching family.

.

The Turner Brothers

Contemporary Erotic Western Romance

Three half-brothers find their own uniquely passionate ways to find the loves of their lives and accept exactly who they are—no holds barred.

.

The Obsidian Series

Sci-Fi Romance

Join a renegade band of telepaths roaming the galaxy to protect and rescue their race from the evil empire intent on destroying them.

.

Planet Valhalla Series

Sci-Fi/Futuristic Erotic Romance

One human female crash lands on a planet full of men descended from the Vikings, one of whom is the King who claims her as his mate— what could possibly go wrong? A sexy romp through the stars with excessive sex, a touch of humor and some very satisfied women…

.

The Triad Series

Sci-Fi/Futuristic Erotic Romance

Welcome to an imaginary world where civilizations, clash against the new and unknown, where telepaths are revered and reviled, and where your destiny can be preordained by a living oracle. Add in a group of super-soldier telepaths rescued from Earth and forming sexual triads for life becomes even more complex and life changing.

.

The Tribute Series

Sci-Fi/Futuristic *Dark* Erotic Romance

To save their planet from extinction the government will demand everything from the condemned few—willingly or not.

"Fans of no-holds-barred erotic portrayals of non- and quasi-consensual encounters will devour this steamy triptych."

– Publishers Weekly

Soul Justice Series

Paranormal Romance

Come and join a San Francisco based secret government department who investigate the monsters under the bed while risking their psychic abilities and even their own lives.

The Tudor Vampire Chronicles

Paranormal Historical Romance

Druids, Vampires and the court of King Henry VIII and his many wives form the backbone of this intriguing series as good fights evil through the first ever female Vampire slayer of her line, Rosalind Llewellyn.

Kurland St. Mary Mysteries

Historical Mystery

Writing as Catherine Lloyd

Join wounded cavalry hero Major Sir Robert Kurland and Lucy Harrington the rector's eldest daughter as they solve crimes in their quiet little village and gradually learn to appreciate each other.

ABOUT KATE PEARCE

New York Times and *USA Today* bestselling author Kate Pearce was born in England in the middle of a large family of girls and quickly found that her imagination was far more interesting than real life. After acquiring a degree in history and barely escaping from the British Civil Service alive, she moved to California and then to Hawaii with her kids and her husband and set about reinventing herself as a romance writer.

She is known for both her unconventional heroes and her joy at subverting romance clichés. In her spare time she self publishes science fiction erotic romance, historical romance, and whatever else she can imagine. You can find Kate at katepearce.com.

amazon.com/author/katepearce

goodreads.com/katepearce

bookbub.com/authors/kate-pearce

facebook.com/KatePearceAuthor

twitter.com/kate4queen

www.ingramcontent.com/pod-product-compliance
Lightning Source LLC
Chambersburg PA
CBHW030638190726
48286CB00008B/2572